Repent in *Haste*

By JOHN P. [P9-BHU-879]

This short novel is the result of a trip made by Mr. Marquand to the West Pacific under the auspices of the United States Navy, and is one of the few serious pieces of fiction so far to appear with the Pacific as a background. Chiefly it is the story of a war marriage. Lieutenant James Boyden, of East Orange, New Jersey, Navy flier, met Daisy, a cute little blonde, at Pensacola. He had been interested in a home town girl, and Daisy was engaged to a man overseas; but it seemed to be love at first sight, so they got married and had a honeymoon. Three months later Boysie, as she called him, was in the Pacific and she was going to have a baby. This is their story, as Briggs the war correspondent learned it from Boysie or pieced together all sorts of silences and stray remarks.

The short flashes of wartime in the Pacific, of the transport planes, Pearl Harbor, Guam, the smoking Japanese island, the transport bringing back the wounded, are selected with an artistic skill which gives this small book both depth and stature; and there are episodes at home through which you meet Boysie's parents and his lonely bride.

This is a story of youth and love and war, highly poignant and convincingly realistic, and few who read it will fail to gain a new insight into the thoughts and environment of the men overseas. It illustrates the abnormal effect of war on people who in other times would lead normal lives.

This story has been
published in *Harper's Magazine*.

Repent in Haste

by John P. Marquand

Haven's End

The Late George Apley

Wickford Point

H. M. Pulham, Esquire

So Little Time

Repent in Haste

John P. Marquand

Repent In Haste

Little, Brown and Company · Boston

1945

FIRST EDITION

Published November 1945

Repent in Haste

I

WILLIAM BRIGGS WAS
sorry that the press boat was alongside to take him
off the support carrier where he had spent the last
three weeks.

The ship's officers and the fliers aboard the
Rogue River were all good kids, most of them boys
just out of college, who had come from diverse
home environments, but who were all much the
same piece of goods. They always referred to each
other as kids, as though to imply their lack of
experience with the civilian world they had left.
They still talked, aboard the *Rogue River*, about
football and about fraternities and blind dates,
when they were not talking about flying and combat. Curiously enough they frequently referred to
the Japanese as kids. They used to say that those

Japanese kids couldn't fly. They hadn't seen a kid out there for the last two weeks who had the word. When Lieutenant Boyden — he was the one they called "Boysie" — had returned from one of the volcano islands, he said those kids came out on the beach and started firing at him with rifles and he went down low and let them have it. You should have seen those kids go down — they had just been kids being trained, that was all.

William Briggs was playing gin rummy in the wardroom when the word came. It was like the wardroom of any other ship, furnished according to wholesale standards — the leatheroid upholstered seats along the bulkhead, the metal-frame mess chairs, the radio and the phonograph records, the shelf of paper-bound books, the green baize covers on the tables, the hot coffee, the electric toaster, and the cups.

"War Correspondent Briggs," the squawker called. "Report on the hangar deck. The press boat coming up forward on the starboard side."

William Briggs rose and put on his helmet.

"Well," he said. "Good-by, boys, I'll be seeing you in church. Do I owe anybody money?"

"So long, Briggsie," they all said. "Don't get your feet wet, Briggsie."

"Come on, Pop," Boysie Boyden said. "I'll see you over the side."

William Briggs smiled at him.

"All right," he said. "Come on, sonny."

Lieutenant Boyden had molasses-colored hair, sandy eyebrows and stubby fingers — he was dumpy, almost fat, but he walked very lightly and easily.

From the rail of the hangar deck the sea looked lead-gray and choppy. The press boat was an LCI camouflaged for the tropics in black and green and yellow. They had thrown lines aboard and she was bobbing and weaving alongside. Lieutenant Boyden was looking at the light gray sky and the darker clouds on the horizon.

"I wish to God it would get blue and keep blue," he said.

William Briggs knew what he meant. An overcast was always dangerous and the radar did not always work.

"You've got that written down now, haven't you?" Boyden asked. "Remember it's East Orange.

If Daisy hasn't got the gas to meet you — but hell, of course the kid will meet you at the station — but if she doesn't, tell the taxi it's the third house down on Maple Street, the only double stucco house, and remember there's a goddam funny tree in front of it, the only one like it there. I don't know what it is — like a kind of a weeping something, but it isn't a weeping willow."

"Maybe it's a Jap tree," Briggs said.

"If it turns out it's a Jap tree," Boyden answered, "you tell Daisy I said yank the goddam thing out. I don't want the kid shoveling sand under any goddam Jap tree." The Officer of the Deck was moving toward them and Boysie spoke more quickly. "And you've got that stuff to give her; and you know what I said to say to the old man."

"I know," Briggs told him. "I'll call as soon as I get to New York."

"If you take the bus through the Holland Tunnel," Boysie said, "they'll let you off at the Socony Filling Station. If Daisy doesn't meet you, just ask for Maple Street."

"Why shouldn't she meet me?" Briggs asked.

"It's what I told you," Boysie answered. "She

does too much at once, poor kid. Tell her I said to take it easy."

"All squared away, sir?" the Officer of the Deck asked.

"Yes," Briggs said. "Let's go." He shook hands with Lieutenant Boyden. "Take care of yourself, son," he said.

"Are you telling me," Boysie answered, "or am I telling you? East Orange, not West Orange."

When Briggs was halfway down the ladder, he looked up and saw Boysie leaning over.

"Watch it, now," Boysie called.

It was a choppy sea, but it was only a question of waiting until the LCI rose on a wave, and then of selecting the right second before she began to roll.

"I'll be seeing you," Boysie called, but his voice was thin and distant, already broken by the wind. The LCI was moving away, and there was no telling whether he would see Boyden or anybody else aboard again. Already the episode of the *Rogue River* was over and everything that Lieutenant James K. Boyden had told him about his love and life was a matter of the past. He assumed that it would be lost in a confusion of other impressions, but instead he could not even forget the tone of Boyden's voice. Its raucous uncultivated quality kept repeating itself in his memory.

In a way it had not been fair, for Briggs had been too clever in piecing together all sorts of silences and stray remarks, so that now he knew too much about Lieutenant Boyden. The knowledge which had been placed in his keeping, carelessly, bit by bit, had become a sort of personal responsibility for which he had never asked. Superficially those revelations had the repetitious mediocrity of the story of the typical American boy, and the same sort of dull normality. It was the sort of thing they printed in the Sunday papers. It might have been the story of Master America.

After all, when Briggs thought of it, Boyden was as dull as his story. In fact, all his aptitudes and perfections made for dullness — he had drawn an 18 on his Schneider, vision 20–20, emotionally stable, organically sound, high school, three years of college, I.Q. 120. He was the best that America had to offer — God's gift to the Navy — initiative, moderate qualities of leadership, the type that could dish it out and take it without cracking under strain,

fine timing under oxygen at 25,000 feet — Boysie
Boyden, the norm of what they wanted, screened
at Pensacola, disciplined by his group, without any
queer ideas — Lieutenant Boyden, Lieutenant America. The only trouble, Briggs was thinking, was
that if you knew too much about anyone, even
someone like Lieutenant Boyden, there began to be
lights and shadows.

For instance, there was the way that Boyden
called everybody "Pops" who was over thirty-
five. Then there was the way he looked at himself in the mirror when he was shaving, just after
he had rinsed the lather from his face and was about
to apply one of those fancy shaving lotions which he
had bought at the Ship's Store. Briggs had caught
him at it sometimes, as you do when you see too
much of someone. Boysie would stand in his skiv-
vies gazing into the mirror, in that complete goldfish privacy of the junior officers' washroom. He
never looked at himself complacently; instead, that
tanned, round face of his wore an expression of
frank surprise, as though he had never seen himself
before.

Sometimes he would move his fingers very

quickly, making little pellets out of the bread at table. He always held his cigarette between his thumb and forefinger, as if he were smoking the last quarter-inch of it, even though it had just been lighted. Then his shirt was always riding out of his trousers. He kept pushing back his chair and loosening his belt and wriggling and pushing his shirt back in again. Those were the things you noticed about someone you knew too well, and somehow they were hard to forget.

And now Boyden and the *Rogue River* were a mile astern, and the press boat was leaving the ships of the screen. The lieutenant commanding the LCI was holding a dispatch. The breeze snatched at it as they stood near the gun platforms amidships.

"We're putting you aboard Transport 240," he said.

"Where is she?" Briggs asked.

"She is in near the island," the lieutenant told him.

Everything since D-day plus 3 had been moving closer to shore. It was about noon when they were near enough to the land to see it clearly. It was a small island, surrounded by the gray silhouettes of all sorts of ships. They formed a patient cordon, that seemed slowly to be crushing out its life. The closeness of the ships to shore showed that there was no longer danger from land batteries, and that the problem now was one of supply and of blasting the pillboxes and the caves. Even at ten thousand yards he could see the smoke rising from the island at points where bombers were hitting it as they peeled out of the clouds. It was obvious that resistance was now confined to the southern end, for he could see the shells from the heavy battleships pounding the higher ground. As they came nearer he could distinguish all the familiar sounds — the concussion of the big guns, the more violent crack of the 5-pounders, the earth-shaking finality of 500-pound bombs, and in between, the antiaircraft and the machine guns and the mortar fire, all forming the usual background of an amphibious operation.

Attack Transport 240 was lying less than a mile offshore. When Briggs climbed up a cargo net near the port bow, the disorder which greeted him was also familiar. They were hoisting aboard the Higgins boats, and the walking wounded were leaning on the rail looking at the shore, and the deck was still littered with equipment. The black sand of the beach lay just in front, with wrecks of landing craft washed against it and with new ships pushing in. He could see the colored markers, and the tanks and jeeps crawling inland. He could see the bursts of mortar shells dropping near a supply dump, and the greenish figures of a reserve Marine battalion moving through the dust. Further inland there was a line of tanks, and he could see the flash from their guns and the sudden spurt of a flame thrower. He had thought it was a great show once and now it was commonplace — only another part of the Pacific war and so much a part of ordinary living that it became puzzling to think of home. You could accept an environment of violence and sudden death but, once you had faced it, it was hard to understand the attitude of those who had not.

That was the great difficulty about going home. There would be that familiar sense of weariness and reaction — that feeling of incredulity and doubt as to whether any of it had really happened. No matter how intelligent you might be, no matter how excellent an observer, there were certain things that could never be explained in terms that anyone at home could grasp, things which even the combat pictures in the newsreels had lost. The individual's response was missing, his unchanging fear and his resigned acceptance.

Briggs was thinking of this at six o'clock that evening while the convoy was moving south. He was standing on the bridge, thinking that it was time for the customary air attack upon the shipping off the island, and like Lieutenant Boyden he did not like the overcast. He wished the sky were blue. If there was any sort of air cover, and he supposed there must be, he could not see it. They were a small convoy, eight empty LSTs that rolled and tossed ahead of them, and then the transport. They were protected by a destroyer and a destroyer escort — not much fire power against an air attack.

Someone had once said that the first fight is always the best fight, and that all of the rest is something more of the same. If you had sailed aboard one transport, you had sailed on them all, for they were all made on a quantity production scale — the bridge, the guns, the wardroom, the crew and the troop quarters were all identical. Even the conversation was a repetition that was cut along the conventional lines of the ship. Briggs was standing with two Marine officers, one with a broken arm and one with a bad leg, and they were talking about the island. They had both been on Tarawa and Saipan and they were comparing the actions. The fire here had been heavier but the Japs were about the same. There was the same Jap officer who ran out of the pillbox waving his sword, and the same wounded Jap who blew himself up with a hand grenade, the same infiltration and the same night attack. There was even the same Jap prisoner who asked to be shot, but who quieted down when they said they would spray him with a flame thrower. There were the questions about such-and-such company, and what had happened to so-and-so, and there were the old remarks about the dead.

In the middle of it there came the rise and fall of General Quarters. The crew were at battle stations already, as they always were at sundown. He heard the destroyer firing, before he saw the plane, but it appeared a few seconds later, diving out of the overcast. It was smoking and the 40-millimeters were tearing through it. It was heading, as far as you could tell, straight for the bridge. There was the old sickening moment of standing and watching, and the old impression of silence in spite of all the noise. Then it veered and its control was gone, and it fell into the sea a hundred yards off the bow. It brought him nothing new. There was the same weakness in the knees, the same dull relief that became sharper and sharper until it expressed itself in the old excited words.

That night before Briggs went to sleep the scenes of the day moved through his mind in a slow orderly sequence — the ships, and the island, and the wreckage, and the transports, and the wounded lying patiently in their berths, and the suicide plane. He knew that there had been an instant on the bridge that would be indelible. That was when he thought again of Lieutenant James K. Boyden. There was that tree in the front yard that was a "weeping something." The house was the only double stucco house on Maple Street. . . . East Orange, not West Orange. . . .

II

WILLIAM BRIGGS HAD first encountered Lieutenant James K. Boyden about eight months before, when people were easier to remember. He had seen so much of the armed forces since then that his faculty for identifying individuals was impaired, and character was lost in the monotony of the uniform. It had grown hard to select any one person from the mass against that restive background. It was better to think of them all as the kids and the older men, as a bulk of expendable human material. It was simpler and safer now to divide them not as friends, each with a personal value, but into the Army, the Marines, and the Seabees; but all of that had been different eight months before.

Now he could view his old enthusiasms with the same faint amusement and the same distrust that

writers who had been out there for a long while
displayed toward the ideas of any new writer just
visiting the theater. Eight months before William
Briggs had been very keenly aware of what was
wrong with war reporting. He had believed it possible to describe people and places and events without resorting to propaganda and without precon-
ceived opinion. He had believed that an observer
could pick out small details, as Tolstoy had done,
or Stendhal. He knew by now that he had been
wrong, or at any rate that he had not been up
to it, and he no longer blamed his contempo-
raries who had tried and failed. It seemed to him by
now that the best writing of the war appeared in
the impersonal reports and citations which simply
accepted everything incredible as everyday, in-
controvertible fact.

When William Briggs was new in the Pacific,
there was an officer at Pearl Harbor assigned to
Public Relations who tried to dig up subjects for
the correspondents to write about — amazing things
that were happening every day, things that they
might otherwise have missed. There were kids
coming into Pearl Harbor every morning, this

commander used to say, who had done the damnedest things you'd ever heard of — kids from Kalamazoo who had crossed the mountains of New Guinea, kids who had been captured by the Lolos in China, kids who had escaped from Japanese prison camps, and who had been with the Philippine guerillas. He had planned a press conference along these lines one morning so that all the correspondents could see some of these kids themselves, and the kids were going to be allowed to talk right off the record. It happened just a week previously that the fast carrier task force of the Third Fleet had made a strike at Formosa. The antiaircraft fire had been exceptionally heavy over certain of the Japanese installations. Shortly after "bombs away" one of those carrier-based torpedo bombers — known as a TEM or Avenger — had received a bad hit. Her pilot kept in formation for a time but when he saw he couldn't make it, he had ditched the plane about a hundred miles offshore. The crew had been out two days on a rubber raft, and now those kids were back at Pearl.

William Briggs had been at Pearl Harbor for

such a short while that he was still glad to stand by the hour looking at the machine shops and the dry-docks and the berths, and this was his first press conference. The meeting was held in one of those Quonset huts, near CINCPAC. There was a table at one end of the room, and then rows of back-breaking metal chairs. When Briggs entered the narrow doorway the low arched room was filling fast, mostly with men but with a few women, too, all in khaki. In spite of their uniforms, the cor-respondents all seemed like civilians. They were beings apart, looked upon with a certain curiosity and suspicion. They were all laughing and talking, slumping down in chairs and lighting cigarettes, and the whole room was filled with bad jokes and smoke. Middle-aged men, and physically unfit younger ones, were pulling scraps of envelopes out of their pockets, and rummaging for pencils and polishing their eyeglasses. They all wore neckties because neckties had to be worn at press con-ferences. You could tell the ones who had been in the West Pacific by the bleached color of their khaki, and by their rough Marine shoes.

A young lieutenant (junior grade) opened a

door at the far end of the room and stepped up to the table and cleared his throat.

"There will be no smoking, please," he said.

His words were followed by a loud derisive titter.

"Who said no smoking?" someone asked.

"You can't get pictures with all this smoke," the officer answered.

"Who said anyone wanted pictures?"

The officer glanced nervously toward the door behind him. "Listen," he said, "the word is the smoking lamp is out."

"Listen, sonny," someone said, "you don't need to put it in sea language. Go on out through the back bulwarks and tell them to start the floor show."

Then the door opened again, and the crowd in the back of the room began standing up to see. A commander, holding some papers, came in first. Then a lieutenant and two crewmen followed him, looking worried and self-conscious, like bad boys being led out before a school. Their foreheads shone with perspiration. Their hair was very carefully brushed. The lieutenant, short and round-faced, came to a halt behind the table and twisted his head from side to side as though his neck hurt him. The first crewman was a rangy, gangly boy who clasped his hands behind his back, and whose throat kept twitching when he swallowed. The other was thin and blond. He was staring straight ahead of him and chewing gum. Photographers were edging up to the table, assuming crouching attitudes.

"No, no, no," the commander said. "We'll take the pictures outside. Are the microphones all right?"

The lieutenant (jg) rushed forward and whispered something and the commander nodded.

"All right," he said. "Let's go. Let's sit down and go."

The pilot and his crew and everyone else sat down, and the commander fiddled with his papers.

"This conference is going on the sound track," he said. "So when anyone has a question, I'd like him to step near a microphone. I imagine everyone knows why we are here. These three men —" he paused and corrected himself, "an officer and two men — are the crew of a bomber from the fast carrier task force of the Third Fleet which struck installations on the Island of Formosa on the morning of — " he glanced at his papers — "the twenty-second. That's right, isn't it, Lieutenant?"

"Yep," the pilot said. "The twenty-second, sir."

"They were hit by flak and the motor began missing. They were obliged to land in the water about a hundred miles out. That's right, isn't it?"

The first crewman swallowed, started to speak and coughed.

"That's near enough, sir," he said.

"All right," the commander said. "Two days later they were picked up by the destroyer *Scaife*. That would be the morning of the twenty-fourth, wouldn't it?"

A chair scraped. A correspondent raised his voice. "What did you say the name of the destroyer was?" he asked.

"*Scaife*," the commander said, "I'll spell it. S-c-a-i-f-e. Got it?"

"What's her commander's name?" someone asked.

The commander glanced at his papers.

"What was his name?" he asked. "Do you remember?"

The three boys looked at each other vaguely.

"It was a sort of a long name, sir," the pilot said. "It had something like grass in it. If someone would say it, I'd remember."

"Was it Snodgrass?" one of the crewmen asked. Everyone laughed and the commander smiled.

"Never mind," he said. "I'll get it for you afterwards. But right now I want you to meet these men, and they'll tell you the whole story better than I can. I just want to say, it's just a normal story out there. We want folks at home to realize that fliers do get picked up. Here's the pilot — Lieutenant James K. Boyden, U.S.N.R. I'll spell it — B-o-y-d-e-n."

"Where's he from?" someone asked.

"From 21 Maple Street, M-a-p-l-e Street," the Commander said, "West Orange, New Jersey."

"East Orange," Lieutenant Boyden said. "Not West Orange."

"Sorry," the commander said, "There's something wrong here — East Orange. And next is the tunnel gunner, Orrin W. Smith, radioman, U.S.N.R.

I don't have to spell Smith, do I? — 21 Parkway Street, Winnetka, Illinois. Got it? Parkway Street. And then the turret gunner, Alfred J. Komiskey, aviation ordnanceman, first class, U.S.N., 28-A — at least, that's the way I've got it — 28-A Thumbull Street. Is that right? Thumbull Street?"

"No, sir," Komiskey said, "Trimble Street."

"Oh," the commander said, "Trimble Street. Boise, Idaho. Got it? Will somebody open some windows here? It's pretty hot. Well, now I'm going to turn the floor over to these boys. Lieutenant Boyden is going to tell his story just the way he told it to me. If anything is off the record, we'll tell you later. Go ahead, Lieutenant."

Lieutenant Boyden stood up and leaned his hands on the table. Then he looked down at his shirt and loosened his belt. His two crewmen gazed at him glassily.

"I guess," Lieutenant Boyden said, "I'm not much at public speaking and there isn't much to tell anyway. There have been lots of kids who have been ditched and on a raft. Rickenbacker was on a raft. You just get out and go for it, that's all."

The commander started to speak and stopped.

There was a long undramatic pause while Lieutenant Boyden stood motionless, staring fixedly at nothing. The room was as humid as a college lecture hall, and Lieutenant Boyden was a disappointing figure — not the birdman type — a short boy, inclined to plumpness, who was already losing the attention of his audience.

"The motor was hit," he said. "Some days you don't get it lucky. I couldn't keep her up in there and I had to give the word we were going to get our feet wet. It kind of threw me when we hit, and I don't remember much. Maybe Smitty — that is Radioman Smith — knows something."

Smitty looked startled and swallowed his gum.

"Lieutenant Boyden sat her down all right," he said.

"Speak up a little louder," the commander told him, and Smith spoke louder.

"He sat her down all right."

"Then what?" the commander asked.

"We just broke out the raft. You pull a couple of things and poops — it inflated, just like they said it would."

There was another dull and clumsy interlude. The

plane was on the sea and there was the raft, but that was all. The three that had been aboard stood behind an embarrassed wall of silence.

"How much time did you have?" someone asked. But none of them appeared to understand the question.

"How long did the plane stay afloat?" the commander asked.

"Maybe thirty seconds, but you don't time it," Smith said. He rubbed his hand across his forehead. "Wasn't it thirty seconds, Lieutenant?"

"How should I know?" Lieutenant Boyden answered. "I was half out."

"Yes," Radioman Smith said more brightly. "He was really out, and do you know what he said when we grabbed him in the water? He said 'Daisy, get me up on the front stoop.' He was really out."

There was another silence while bodies shifted uneasily on the hard seats and feet scraped on the floor. The boys behind the table might have been speaking in some foreign language for all they were able to convey. The plane had sunk in the Pacific, one of those orange-colored rafts had inflated itself — poops! Those boys did not seem older or wiser.

No fine thoughts had appeared to go through their heads in the struggle for survival.

"Who was Daisy?" someone asked.

"That's my wife," Lieutenant Boyden said. "Mrs. James K. Boyden, 21 Maple Street, East Orange, New Jersey."

"Any children?"

"James K. Boyden, Jr., five months," the lieutenant said.

"So you were thinking of her out there," — it was a woman's voice — "and the little boy."

"I wouldn't know," Lieutenant Boyden said. "Maybe I was thinking that Daisy and I, that is, Mrs. Boyden, had been out dancing somewhere and I had taken three or four too many and she was helping me up the steps. I wouldn't know. Then I heard that fellow there — Smitty — say 'get the hell ahold of him' and then I was on the raft. When I woke up we were still on it. The kids were breaking out gadgets. There are a lot of gadgets on those rafts. Then the next morning a plane spotted us, and the morning after, a can came up. We were really glad to see that can. When I got aboard, I said to the Skipper — 'Let's get the heck out of here.' It was enemy waters, but the old man wanted to cruise a while. We were really frightened on that can."

"Well, I guess that's about all," the commander said. "And I know that everybody here is very grateful for hearing your own story in your own words. There may be a few points and a little more color, if anyone wants to gather around and ask questions, but I'm sure we're all very grateful, so thanks a lot."

The chairs scraped across the floor, and there was a perfunctory round of applause. A few of the correspondents gathered around the fliers by the table, but most of them walked out, and William Briggs walked with them into the bright Hawaiian sunlight. He knew he had heard all there was to hear. Those boys would never be able to put their thoughts into words. He was as embarrassed as they had been, by that indecent public exposure.

He could imagine already the version of it that would reach home.

This morning at Naval Headquarters three young fliers of the Carrier Force of the Third Fleet added in their own words another epic to the legends of the sea. They were Lieutenant James K. Boyden, U.S.N.R., pilot, East Orange, New Jersey, his turret gunner, Alfred J. Komiskey, Boise, Idaho, and his tunnel gunner, Orrin W. Smith of Winnetka, Illinois. Looking at these three lads standing modestly at their first press conference, it was indeed difficult to visualize that they had crashed in the ocean, and had been picked up from a raft only two days previously. Now, no worse for their ducking, they chatted and reminisced almost gaily about sharks and wind and drift, and about their thoughts of home.

"I was more frightened when I was aboard the destroyer that picked me up," Pilot Boyden said, with a merry twinkle, and his two crew members joined in the laugh that followed. . . .

It was a fair sample of many press conferences, and most of them added up to just as little. Yet William Briggs wondered, at the time, whether it might not all have been different if that interview had not been so artificially contrived. If he had seen Lieutenant Boyden alone, for example, if they could have taken a drink or two together, the lieutenant might not have been inarticulate. He thought of Kipling and the three soldiers, and of Owen Wister and the Virginian. It was a question of the personal touch, he thought — but then there was no basis for companionship between himself and Lieutenant Boyden. It never occurred to him that he would ever see the lieutenant again.

III

WHEN WILLIAM BRIGGS had agreed to go out to the Pacific for a syndicate, he was confident that he would do as well as most. He was rated above the average among special feature writers, although he had never been foolish enough to have illusions that his work possessed a high literary quality. He had been in Paris in 1940 and had been in London during the blitz. He had a clear perspective and a retentive memory, but now, when the time had arrived to produce some sort of article, for almost the first time in his experience he had no concrete ideas.

Beneath the window of his room at the Moana Hotel that evening the beach was deserted, except for three small Hawaiian boys in bathing trunks. When a wave broke, they would run for it, fall flat and glide over two inches of water without ever once scratching their bellies. Now that the darkness was coming on, quickly, as it always did out there, a detail of troops arrived on the seawall and began setting up a machine gun. Somehow these extraneous sights made William Briggs feel lost and unsure of himself. He recalled what an admiral had said to him that afternoon at Pearl Harbor, something about everyone's being in one big team, and he had not yet become resigned to that almost universal habit of generals and admirals — explaining war in terms of a football game. It was time for him to write a letter home.

"Dear Meg," he wrote. ". . . I got here three days ago and I suppose I shall be moving out before long, but I should like to see the show here first. It is all pretty confusing and crowded. Someone said this afternoon that we are all one big team. . . ."

When he went downstairs to mail his letter, everyone else was going somewhere, and most of that coming and going was arranged for in a vast pattern and he was no part of it. He was under his own volition to come or go — to take it or leave it. He felt like a neutral observer.

In the courtyard that faced the sea he came upon a group of professional entertainers playing Hawaiian music. Colored electric lights were strung beneath the branches of a banyan tree and the artists were gathered on a porch. As he peered over the heads of the crowd that stood listening, the music stopped. A young man with marcelled hair, clad in white ducks and a batik sports shirt, took his place before a shining microphone and read a piece from a sheet of paper in a mellifluous radio announcer's voice.

"This is the Friendly Voice of Hawaii calling the Mainland," he was saying. "And before we continue our program of island songs and fantasy, some of your boys here with us are going to step up and say a few words to the folks at home. First we have Pharmacist's Mate Joe McCloskey. His folks are waiting at Utica, New York, to hear his voice. Step up here, Joe. Tell them how you are, Joe."

Pharmacist's Mate McCloskey rubbed the palms of his hands upon his trousers and swung backward on his heels and then forward to his toes.

"How long have you been out here, Joe?"

"I've been stationed here for eight months," he said.

The announcer clapped him on the back. "Come on, Joe. The folks are waiting in Utica, New York," he said. "And while Joe is thinking what to say I'll tell you he's looking fine. He's put on weight and he's got a good suntan and not from any ultra-violet lamp."

The announcer thrust a piece of paper into McCloskey's hand and McCloskey began to read.

"Hullo, folks," McCloskey said. "Hullo, Pa — Ma — and everybody. I want you to know I'm fine and I like it here. Everybody treats us boys right on this old rock. I want to say 'hullo' to the old gang, if any of the old gang is left, and I particularly want to say 'hullo' to a certain party, and I guess you know who I mean, and I hope she is listening to me now. Good-by now."

"Well, that's fine, Joe," the announcer said. "And now stepping up is Private First Class Norman Judkins, from Green Lake, Ohio, and Norman is looking fine, too. How long have you been with us, Norman?"

William Briggs's attention was distracted by an

impolite sound, just beside him, and he was surprised to find that he was standing next to Lieutenant Boyden. The red glare of the electric-light bulbs shone on the lieutenant's face. Briggs would never have spoken if Boyden had not spoken first. He had a certain feeling of reluctance at presuming to intrude, since he was a not a member of the team.

"That poor kid must be goddam lonely," Lieutenant Boyden said, "to face up to anything like that."

William Briggs remembered that he was pleased and flattered when Lieutenant Boyden addressed him.

"Yes," he answered, "it's a long way from Utica."

Lieutenant Boyden nodded. "That isn't what I meant," he said. "I had to do the same thing myself this morning in front of a whole goddam room."

"I know," Briggs said. "I heard you," and he felt apologetic.

This accidental meeting was exactly the sort of opportunity that he had wanted. They had all told him that the thing to do was to chat with some of the kids and get their point of view, and here was

Lieutenant Boyden, but the difficulty was that there was nothing to chat about.

"Cripes," Lieutenant Boyden said. "I thought you were in the Army, Pop."

"It's these electric lights," Briggs said, and then, without knowing exactly why, he felt it was necessary to explain himself. "I'm too old to fight in this war. I just came out to do a little writing. That was quite a talk you gave this morning."

"It was lousy," Boyden answered. "Don't kid me, Pop."

"It must have been hard standing up there," Briggs began. He realized that the conversation was getting nowhere, and he was glad that he did not have to go on with it.

"There's some rye up in the room," Boyden said. "I guess it's time I got back to it. Well, so long — unless you could do with a drink."

"Why, thanks," Briggs told him. "If it wouldn't bother you."

"Cripes," Boyden answered. "Nothing bothers me. That's how I keep alive."

It was only in the elevator when they were going up to Lieutenant Boyden's room that Briggs saw that he was drunk. It did not appear in his walk and speech as much as in his defenseless candor.

"Yes," Boyden said. "Don't let anything bother you. There used to be a friend of mine on the old *Lex* who said that. Why bother?"

He led the way down the hall with quick brisk steps.

"Now, what the hell was the number?" he asked.

Boyden ran his hands through his pockets and produced a key. He pushed aside some empty bottles, unlocked a door and turned on the light. Everything in the room had been thrown every which way. There were three beds. The contents of three sea-bags were strewn across the floor. The bureau was covered with bottles and containers of melted ice. Towels, uniforms, bathing trunks and toilet articles were strewn across the beds and two lieutenants (jg) who were also pilots were sprawled on the beds, dead to the world.

"Nobody to talk to," Lieutenant Boyden said. "That's why I came downstairs." He picked up a bottle from the bureau and filled two glasses. "Well, here's looking at you, Pop. Move their legs over and sit down." William Briggs sat down carefully.

"Happy days," he said.

Lieutenant Boyden took off his tie and pulled off his shirt. His undershirt with its quarter-length sleeves had holes in it that displayed ragged sections of the lieutenant's plump, muscular torso. The lieutenant's eyes were gray-blue and round and his mouth, rather a large mouth, was half open, as though he were not sure that he had heard correctly.

"What's that you said?" he asked.

"I said, 'Happy days,'" Briggs answered.

Lieutenant Boyden brushed some shirts and socks off a chair.

"Oh, yeh, pardon me, Happy days," he said. "Don't mind the kids. Those two always pass out early."

He raised his glass, threw his head back, and finished half of it. William Briggs sat on the edge of the bed trying to think of something to say, while the sound of music from the courtyard came through the open window.

Just before he had left New York, when he had come back to the apartment at five one afternoon, he had found his daughter Clara giving a tea-party for her dolls, and she had asked him to sit on the floor beside the little table. Curiously enough, he was now experiencing the same sense of unreality, the same embarrassed effort to adjust himself to the unfamiliar, the same attempt to recapture something which he had lost. Now, instead of a doll's teacup, he was holding half a glass of raw rye whiskey. Instead of dolls, he was on a bed beside two insensible young officers. Instead of Clara, he was talking to a drunken lieutenant.

"There used to be a correspondent on the old *Lex*," Lieutenant Boyden said. "What's his name? I don't remember. What's your assignment, Pop?"

Before he answered, Briggs finished his drink, but the drink made it no better.

"I'm going out with a task force. What's going to happen to you?"

Lieutenant Boyden had been looking at him and past him, and now his eyes focused unwinking on William Briggs.

"Two days' leave. Doctors. Reassignment. You've just come out, haven't you?"

"How can you tell that?" William Briggs asked.

"Hell!" Lieutenant Boyden told him. "Anyone can tell them when they're new. How's it back there? How's New York?"

"Just about the same," Briggs answered, "not so many lights."

Lieutenant Boyden finished his drink and reached for the bottle.

"The other night I heard a New York broadcast," he said. "Sometimes I get to thinking, although I don't let it bother me. That's my motto, you understand. Don't let anything bother. It was called 'Do Our Boys Know What We Are Fighting For?' I sometimes wonder why they don't get over it."

"How do you mean?" William Briggs asked.

He could see that Lieutenant Boyden was struggling with an abstract idea, and it was almost a physical effort. He set his glass on the corner of the writing table, beside some shaving implements, and grasped both knees with his plump hard hands.

"I mean why the heck should it bother them, if we're in here pitching. We're in here pitching, aren't we?"

In his still fresh enthusiasm William Briggs was trying to translate the scene into the terms of a human-interest story — the clear-eyed young officer speaking confidently of his ideals. Briggs was still thinking of war aims and of why people fought and died. It was true that the atmosphere was not exactly suitable, with two young drunks on the bed, and instead of being clear-eyed, Lieutenant Boyden was having trouble with his eyesight and his syllables. When he reached for his glass again, his arm hit the bottle. It tipped sideways toward the floor, but there was still nothing the matter with the boy's timing. He caught it when it was in mid-air and laughed.

"Baby, that was close," he said.

Briggs was thinking it would be quite possible to place this conversation in a more palatable setting — the beach — the sun — Boyden back from a long swim, with a trimmer figure and full of the zest of living, defining ingenuously his philosophy.

"Well, now you've brought the subject up — what are you fighting for?" Briggs asked.

Boyden scratched his skin under his undershirt.

"I think I'm getting the itch," he said.

"Go ahead," Briggs said, "never mind the itch. What are you fighting for?"

Boyden stopped scratching and put his hands back on his knees.

"What the hell else is there to do?" he asked. "We're in here pitching, aren't we? You get used to it, Pop. What else is there to do?"

"Let's put it another way," Briggs said.

"What other way?" Boyden asked.

"I mean," Briggs said, "*why* do you do it? And don't say 'What else is there to do?' "

"Well, that's still the answer, isn't it?" Boyden said. "You wouldn't let the gang down, would you? That's the word — don't let down the gang."

"How long have you been out here?" Briggs asked.

"Since late summer of '43."

"That's quite a while."

"Yeh," Boyden said. "If I last much longer, they'll begin to call me Pops."

"Did you always feel this way?" Briggs asked.

"What way?"

"The way you feel now."

Boyden was having difficulty with the line of thought.

"If I hadn't," Boyden said, "I'd have washed out. What d'you think I am, Pops, emotionally unstable?"

"No," Briggs told him, "I wouldn't say you were."

Lieutenant Boyden picked up the bottle and crossed the room to where Briggs was sitting. He swayed with his first step, then regained his balance and threaded his way around the sea-bags neatly and easily.

"Kill her off, Pop," Boyden said. "We've got to kill her off."

"Thanks, haven't you had about enough?" Briggs asked.

"No," Boyden answered, "you never can tell when you'll get it next. I'll tell you something — now we're on the subject. The thing is not to think too much. I've seen a lot of kids thinking, especially the new kids, and it isn't normal."

"I don't see how you can help it," Briggs said.

"I'll tell you," Boyden answered. "Take torpedoes. You go in over the water, maybe as low as fifty feet. You let it go when you're two hundred yards away. It's all right when you're doing it, if you don't get thinking first. Just climb in and say a little prayer."

"You pray, do you?" Briggs asked.

"Praying's better than thinking, isn't it?" Boyden answered. "But I'll tell you, now we're on the subject. There are times when it doesn't hurt to let yourself go, and think."

"When?" Briggs asked.

"At a time like this," Boyden said. "You've got me thinking."

"What do you think about?" Briggs asked.

Boyden looked up at the ceiling and reached for the bottle again.

"Home," he said. "This just about kills it. My kid, and when I was a kid — all those things. Only there's one thing you've got to remember. This is one place and that's another. You don't want to get the two of them mixed up. Do you know what I mean? I don't know what they're doing and they don't know what I'm doing. That kind of thinking's all right — that's normal; and me, I'm very normal, or else I'd be washed out."

"So you think about home and when you were a kid," Briggs said.

"I make it into a kind of a story in my mind," Boyden answered, "at a time like this."

But against that background William Briggs

could not help mixing the two things together —
Lieutenant Boyden in his undershirt and the Boyden back home.

"And there's another thing I've learned, Pops,"
Boyden said, "out here, you don't want to get liking
anyone too much. Be pals with the crowd, but
don't like them too much, because what's the good
in it? You get to liking a kid and it upsets you
when he dies. But it's all right at a time like this
when you have a little time. It's normal to be more
friendly." He pointed toward the bed. "Now, those
kids there are the best damn kids." He picked up
the bottle and it was empty. He tossed it on the
floor. "They're the same as any kids back home."

As time went on, William Briggs understood
what Boyden meant. It was safer not to get too
interested in anyone out there. It was better simply
to know everyone superficially and to let it go at
that. You could never tell who would come or who
would go. New faces appeared from Washington
and old faces left for shore duty. Submarine so-
and-so was overdue and presumed lost, and the
next-of-kin were notified. You would board a ship
and have coffee in the wardroom and the next

morning she would have pulled out — you never knew just where. You would go out with a DE and watch the rocket practice, and talk about base-ball and the Civil War, and you might never see those boys again; but on the other hand, perhaps at some officers' club on some island when the bar was open, you would see a face and there would be the skipper of that same DE, or the transport pilot who had let you sit beside him in the co-pilot's chair for an hour or so when you flew out to Guam.

It was a long while before he saw Boyden again after those few days they had been together at Honolulu. It was not until Briggs had been assigned to the support carrier *Rogue River* off Ulithi and the whole aspect of the war had changed, and Briggs himself had changed in many ways.

The word was that this rendezvous was going to be the beginning of the biggest show yet. There was the greatest concentration of warships that the world had ever seen. They extended over the rims of the horizon, so many that he wondered how an organization could exist that could supply and group and count them and send them on their way.

At night the ocean was dotted with their lights, shining contemptuously although the Japanese at Yap were only a few hundred miles to the south. Briggs had just climbed aboard the support carrier and before he had even reported to the Officer of the Deck he came face to face with Boyden on the hangar deck. Boyden looked well and rested, without a new line on his face.

"Hullo, Pops," he said, "are you going north on this party?"

"Yes," Briggs said, "and then I'm heading home."

"Home?" Boyden repeated.

"Just for a month or six weeks," Briggs told him.

"Well, keep your fingers crossed, and wash behind your ears, and maybe you'll make it," Boyden said.

"Where's Smitty?" Briggs asked him.

"Smitty?" Boyden repeated. "That kid's gone."

"Gone where?" Briggs started to ask, but then he realized where Smitty had gone.

"He was a good kid," Boyden said. "He wasn't with us, but we got the word."

"Where's the other one?" Briggs asked. "The one from Boise, Idaho?"

Boyden laughed.

"Back at Pearl," he said — "28–A Trimble Street, not Thumbull Street, remember?"

It had been quite a while but Briggs remembered. He was transferred to Transport 240 three weeks later.

IV

IT WAS A FINE CLEAR DAY, and very much warmer than it had been six hundred miles up north, when Briggs got back to Guam. Transport 240 steamed through the narrow entrance of Apra harbor, passing the steep cliffs to starboard with their rich vegetation. The sunlight gave the water over the coral reefs to port tints of green and violet. They were busy blowing out the coral with dynamite and the charges went off like bombs, blowing geysers of water up toward the light blue sky. There were several new drydocks and dozens of new berths.

The transport edged close to a sand and coral mole, where a column of ambulances was lined up to take off the wounded. Briggs was standing on the bridge with the chaplain, who had been speaking of a group of gravely wounded in the wardroom.

"Those boys," the chaplain said, "have never had a chance to live."

He was partially right, but out there time possessed all sorts of dimensions and a good many of the boys who were dying had experienced years in terms of minutes.

In some ways Guam was like an oil town in Oklahoma. The Navy and the Army had certainly struck it rich in terms of the taxpapers' money. Nothing was too good for Guam, nothing too expensive, because there was a war. Once Congress had jibbed at a few millions for harbor improvements, but now the sky was the limit. They had carved out motor highways and they were building more. They were leveling off the tops of the hills, and building towns for the natives beside the ruins of Agana. The B.O.Q.'s up on the hill at CINCPAC — called Bachelor Officers' Quarters as though different accommodations for married officers existed there — were as comfortable and very much quieter than the B.O.Q.'s at Pearl Harbor. The Officers' Mess was established in one Quonset hut with tables and silver for captains or better, and the Officers' Club had already opened in another.

Briggs recalled that, aboard the *Rogue River*, when the word came that the Marines had raised the flag on Surabachi, someone had said they would be building the Officers' Club up there tomorrow.

Guam was still enough of a frontier so that the club was like a frontier bar, with a board counter where the drinks were being sold, and a long mess table covered with empty beer cans. The benches were crowded when Briggs came in. Army, Marine and Naval officers, Red Cross men and correspondents, were all there talking at once, because the day was over. It was the crossroads to anywhere. You talked and drank your beer and left, and only God and Headquarters knew whether you would come back again.

The passengers were already climbing into the black shadows of the cabin when Briggs reached his plane next morning — first the captains, then the commanders, according to rank, like animals entering the Ark. Inside the two rows of bucket seats faced each other. The life rafts were packed and the thermos of coffee was ready for the evening meal.

The plane was gaining altitude and getting on its course. The palms, the deep green shining leaves of the breadfruit trees, and the roads and the Quonset huts grew smaller. They were well above the island now, so that he could look into the gorges where there were still pockets of Japanese. Soon there would be nothing but cloud and water until they let down at Kwajalein that night.

Passengers balancing on their bucket seats, with angles of aluminum to lean against, formed a cross section of all the Pacific services — Army and Navy fliers going back to join new groups, a submarine lieutenant commander, a Navy captain from the Headquarters Staff, a yeoman and three electronic specialists, a captain of the Marines recovering from malaria, three paratroopers, a middle-aged officer from the Seabees, an Army lieutenant with the Silver Star, a lieutenant (jg) carrying dispatches. Some of them had pulled out cigarettes. Some were reading paper-covered detective stories, and others were simply thinking. One might have learned a great deal about the war if they had only spoken their thoughts, but they were silent. It was only in the war books that fliers and PT boys really ever talked. Suppose everyone on the seats opposite had begun speaking as they did in one of those books "as told to Bill Sykes or Spike Mahaffey." For some reason all those authors signed their names in abbreviation.

A group of fresh-faced, happy-go-lucky fellows, tanned by the sun and inured to the hardships in the Pacific, gathered about this reporter in a jovial little knot, as the plane winged its way from Guam to Kwajalein.

"You ought to see the going-over the cans gave us off Yokohama," the big submariner began.

"They shook the paint off the old pipe," his companion interjected, taking up the tale.

"Then we made a pass at that sampan," the little flier interrupted brightly.

"I didn't think I'd ever see Junior again," the other flier ejaculated laughingly.

"You boys ought to have seen it at Leyte," the tank man interrupted, unwilling to be left out.

"It was really rugged at Leyte," the paratrooper volunteered. "We really hit the silk."

All those boys were talking so fast that this reporter found it difficult to unravel their skein of experience.

That was the way it went in those war books, but William Briggs had never heard them talk like that.

About the time that the sun was setting, he was thinking that Lieutenant Boyden was a fair common denominator for all those figures seated opposite. He was thinking of Boyden as a baby and as a little boy, as a composite of those photographs of children that everyone carried in wallets or pasted sometimes on the scabbards of their dirks. It was difficult to see across the plane now that it was getting dark. The door of the crew's compartment opened and one of the crew walked slowly down to the tail, giving the word from the plane commander. They were going to proceed blacked out — no lights, no more cigarettes. In a little while there was nothing in the plane but darkness.

Briggs had once told Lieutenant Boyden that he had first seen New York in 1922 in the spring vacation of his junior year at Dartmouth and Boyden had said it was funny the way things happened. That was the very year that Boyden had been born — right there in New York City. There was Briggs, a college man, and Boyden drinking milk. Boyden had said that his father, Philip Boyden, had a job with a printing and engraving company, and had married a girl in the office named Carrie Hines, who used to work on lay-outs. The old man, Lieutenant Boyden said, had been in one of the Infantry Regiments of the old 77th in the last war, shortly after he had graduated from Hamilton College. Boyden's mother must have been a fairly pretty girl, and on the whole, the marriage could not have worked out badly. There was one thing the Boydens had always wanted and that was a home of their own and when the boy was born they moved out to East Orange to a new and quite badly built house which they could pay for finally just like rent.

Boyden must have passed through the usual conventional middle-class childhood, and when William Briggs tried to relive the pattern of it, as he sat there in the dark listening to the motors, its simplicity and security conveyed an extraordinary sense of peace. There was so much in those days that one always took for granted. There was a sense of routine activity which included a lively instinct for acquisition usually applied to marbles, stamps, or rabbits. It must all have had some purpose.

"I used to have the damnedest tumbler pigeons." Briggs's memory of Lieutenant Boyden's voice chimed in with the motors. "The old man helped me fix them up in the back yard, and Susie was always trying to get in at them. By God, you should have seen them drop, just as though you'd got a bead on them and let them have it. . . . The boys used to pick on me because I was kind of fat." It was Boyden's voice again. "Until I took two of them on at once. They licked me but I marked them up. I wasn't so bad for my weight. I played end once in the game against Summit High."

You could have put it all together into a sort of common reservoir of national thought. Despite their disparity in age, he and Boyden must have shared the same superstitions, and the same vulgar word-of-mouth beliefs. They both must have read the *American Boy* magazine, and *The Adventures of Frank Merriwell*, and the works of the late Ralph Henry Barbour. They both must have learned not to lie, and not to go back on the crowd. No matter who you might be, you were exposed to certain precepts of conduct. You learned the Lord's Prayer, and that Christ had risen from the dead, and that you must pledge allegiance to the flag, and that we had fought the British and gained our independence because we could lick anybody in the world. You picked up a few frontier notions as a boy scout or from a visit to a summer camp, and also a few inaccuracies about sex. Those were the things you learned so well that all subsequent knowledge was built on their plain foundation stones. You could disbelieve parts of it afterwards, but you could not forget.

"The old man used to make gadgets down in the cellar on Saturdays when he was home." It was Boyden's voice again. "He had a lathe and a jig saw. He made a doll's house for Susie. Boy, it was really quite a house. I made a plane down there — the kind you bought knocked down, but you had to be some kid to put one of those together. You wound it on elastics, and poops — you let it go."

There would be, if Briggs cared to fill in the blank spaces, a front lawn that ran down to a concrete sidewalk, and a flower border with peonies and iris and hollyhocks, and a vine of Indian pipe that climbed along the uprights of the front porch. There would be the house itself — a ten-thousand-dollar wooden type of house that was known as Colonial — and beside it two strips of concrete leading to the garage in back, where the pigeons lived behind their netting and where the clotheslines were stretched.

"Sundays we would go out in the car, Ma and Susie — all of us. The old man taught me to drive it when I was sixteen. He was great at fixing up a flivver. He can still make them go, and he and my mother played a pretty good game of bridge. When he got more in the chips, he joined the golf club because that was the thing to do, but he never had the jack to go there much."

You could place them easily enough from such remarks of Boyden's. His father would be in the category of a minor executive with an annual income of perhaps eight thousand dollars, one of those thousands of commuters who streamed out of the ferry slip into downtown New York each weekday.

"Ma played the piano some. Susie used to take music lessons."

They always did have music lessons in Boyden's walk of life.

There were antimacassars on the parlor chairs and the radio had Jacobean legs and an inlaid front and the gas stove would cook without watching and there was an automatic electric toaster and an electric percolator in the breakfast nook. Boyden always spoke of all those things as though they were in front of him and each endowed with a peculiar importance. He could also remember the titles of the books in the glass-covered bookcase in the parlor. It was of golden oak and the key was kept in a white glass vase on the piano. There was a set of Conrad which the girls in the office had given his mother as a wedding present, and *Specimens of Famous Oratory*, and then some of his father's college books, such as *An Introduction to Geology*, Chaucer, Shakespeare in two volumes, and a French Dictionary.

His own room was upstairs over the kitchen. That was where he kept his own stuff and Briggs could guess what it was, even before Boyden told of it. An air rifle, a fielder's mitt, a box of electric gadgets, schoolbooks, a colored print by Maxfield Parrish of a tall blonde talking to a knight in front of a medieval castle; and later, a photograph of his high school class, and later still, a picture of the crowd in front of his frat house. When Boyden went back to the States on his only leave, he had gone upstairs to look at his room and, Boyden said, it had given him quite a bang. There had been no time to move any of it to his new place, but some-day when this show got over, he was going to have a place something like a rumpus room but not exactly, where he could take friends for a drink, and he was going to have a lot of his old stuff in it. He was going to collect a lot of old snapshots of kids, the boys and girls he used to know. Daisy had never cared about those things, because she was always doing too much at once, but someday he was going to get all his things together and sort them out and throw away the stuff he did not want, such as girls' letters. There was no use keeping too much kid's stuff around too long.

There was the drugstore on the corner down by the carline, and the movie house and the moun-tain where you could walk along the ridge through the woods and see New York City.

"Wasn't there a girl next door?" Briggs had asked him once.

There had not been a girl next door. She had lived three doors down on the other side of the street and her name was Verna May Lewis. Mr. Lewis had something to do with a public utility company and Mrs. Lewis and Boyden's mother be-

longed to the Woman's Club, and they both were
in the Altar Guild at the Episcopal church, but
he had never noticed Verna May much. Sometimes in high school he would walk down the
street with her, but the truth was that he was
afraid of girls when he was a kid, shy; and besides
his mother and everyone else seemed to expect him
to go around with Verna May.

"Wouldn't it be nice," his mother used to say,
"to ask Verna May over to supper, Jimmy? And
then you two could go to the moving pictures."

Then Susie would begin to giggle, and his father
would say, "Yes, why don't you take Verna to the
pictures, Jim?"

Now anyone should have known what people
would say, if you went around with one girl. He
wanted it to be very clear that there was nothing
whatsoever between him and Verna May. His best
friend was a kid named Sam Tilton, and God
knows where Sam was now; but Sam was the one
who taught him a good deal about women. Sometimes he and Sam would take some of the girls in
school out in Sam's father's car, and there would
naturally be a certain amount of petting and neck-

ing — nothing very serious (you know the way kids are) but he never took Verna May on any of those rides. Verna didn't go around with that crowd; besides, Mrs. Lewis would have heard of it and Mrs. Lewis would have told the family and then there would have been hell to pay; besides, Verna would have thought it all meant something, and of course a little necking did not mean anything at all.

There was one thing that impressed Briggs — the unblemished mediocrity of that boyhood and youth, so complete a tribute to environment.

"Did you ever get to thinking what anything was about?" Briggs had asked Boyden once.

"What the hell do you mean, what anything was about?" Boyden answered.

Of course Briggs had meant the outside world, its economic and political tumult and the events that indicated the end of peace, but Boyden said that there had not been any time to think of any of that stuff. Professors up at college kept talking about that stuff, but Boyden's idea had always been to let them and Mr. Roosevelt do the worrying, and any kids who began figuring on those angles

were in the queer bunch. The family had taken out
educational insurance so that he could go to college, and he was having too tough a time with
French and chemistry and ancient history to worry
about any more deep stuff. He was doing what
everyone was doing and it took up all his time.
There was the fraternity rush season and he had to
put his mind on whether he ought to go Sigma Delt
or Gamma Phi, and besides there were all the college sports like football, for instance — and that
was a full job in itself — let alone passing the exams.
He was light for college football but he was quick
on his feet and he had played in the last quarter of
the game against Summit High. Besides, he was
learning quite a lot about life, and that took a lot
of thinking. It wasn't normal not to go out with
the crowd, where there was a juke box and a few
drinks, and all that sort of business used up a lot
of energy. It took real work just trying to learn
and to get things straight without worrying what
Krauts and Frogs and Wops and sharecroppers
were doing. You had to learn how to tell a real Joe
from a drip, for instance, and how far you could
go with a certain type of girl.

"Believe me," Boyden said, "a kid has a lot to learn, particularly an American kid."

You had to know all those things he was talking about, and besides you had to get to develop some sort of a line so you wouldn't be a drip yourself. You had to learn the swing steps and the proper clothes, if you wanted to keep up with the crowd — and all of that was a full-time job in itself — let alone everything else that everyone kept pushing at you.

"Didn't you ever plan what you were going to do?" Briggs had asked him.

"Do?" Boyden said. "Believe me, I was doing plenty, Pop."

Of course, Boyden said, you had to get around to that sort of thing sometime. You could cope with it in your last year at college but there wasn't any last year, because the war had busted it all up. Besides you had to get set first, and you had to learn all these other things and look around. Boyden's idea was that maybe he would have liked to get a job traveling to places like the pictures in the *National Geographic Magazine*, but he was fed up on those places now till they were running out his ears. Anyhow, there were other matters much more important to an American kid than what he was going to do, because you always ended by doing something. Love was more important. There was a problem that a kid simply had to work out for himself.

"It's a funny thing — love," Boyden said.

"Yes," Briggs repeated after him, "it's a funny thing — love."

All right, you could be cynical about it if you were an old guy and had worked it out, but the funny thing about love was you couldn't tell what was real love and what wasn't, not until it was all over and you began loving somebody else. This wasn't just Boyden's own experience either. In fact he knew now that everything that had happened to him was perfectly normal because he had compared notes with a lot of other kids. Of course, he had thought he was in love a couple times before it got serious, once with a little number back in high school, and once with the daughter of a professor of physics in Troy, New York, but neither of these was serious. The first time that he was positive that he was in love, so that it fooled him, was the Christmas vacation of his sophomore year, and Boyden said that this was the way it happened.

No sooner had he got to East Orange and got his stuff up to his room than his mother came knocking on the door. She was just back from the Altar Guild where they had been working on floral plans for the Christmas services. She gave him a big kiss and said how well he looked. It was a funny thing that you never felt grown up when you were with your mother, and that was not just his individual experience either.

"Jimmy," she said, "I've accepted an invitation for you tonight to go to Verna May's birthday party."

He had been to Verna's party last year and he imagined that there would be a cake and musical chairs just as though they were all still kids.

"But Jimmy," his mother said. "You know you are very fond of Verna May."

There was no way of getting out of it, because his mother and Mrs. Lewis were dear friends and both in the Woman's Club, so he put on his tux and walked across the street with Susie, who was just fifteen and old enough to go.

"Jimmy's fond of Verna May," Susie kept saying. "Jimmy's fond of Verna May." There was no use telling Susie to shut up. In fact, it was his experience that you never got anywhere arguing with women. It was easier to take it and walk along and whistle a tune.

He was just beginning to learn that some people were more in the chips than other people, but it never bothered him the way it did some other kids. He was just as good as anybody else, and he could make all the dough he wanted as soon as he got around to it. That was why going to a home like the Lewis home never troubled him, although it was pretty big, with a downstairs lavatory just off where you hang your coats, and a sun porch and a library besides a living room. No matter how big those houses were in the Oranges, and no matter how much jack the old people had, they were always looking for an extra man at parties — particularly a college man with a good line who was good on his feet. There was quite a crowd at the Lewises', even some kids from Llewellyn Park. The dining-room table was all covered with little cakes and sandwiches and coffee, and there was a fruit punch and coke and ginger ale, and even some sherry. It was a lot better party than he thought it was going to be, if they just hadn't played paper games and stuff like "Twenty Questions."

When he saw Verna May standing in the living room talking to some Princeton and Yale drips, it amazed him that he had never realized what a cute little trick she was. It all went to prove that you could never tell how a kid would turn out until she started working on herself. Verna May was a little taller than he was and that was something that had always put him off her, but now it did not matter, because she had a new hair-do that made her look dark and slinky, and lipstick, and a sort of yellow-green pastel party dress.

"Hi, Verna," he said, "how's tricks?" or something like that, just a casual opening line. Somehow when you liked a girl, it was his experience that in some way she could tell it and you also could tell in some way, right off, whether she liked having you like her. That was the way it was right off with him and Verna May.

"I never knew you liked me until that night," she told him.

That was one of the peculiar things about love, whether it was real or not, you always thought you had always liked someone that you thought you were in love with, and that was just what Verna May said.

"Of course, I always liked you subconsciously, Jimmy, but you were *so* sophisticated that night."

And that was exactly the way he had felt about her, too. She was sophisticated. She was sophisticated the next night when he kissed her after he had taken her to the movies.

"We mustn't be too silly, Jimmy dear," she said.

In his experience you could always tell after you had kissed a girl whether you wanted to go on with it. There was only one thing about Verna May that bothered him — or maybe there were two things. She seemed to be too sure about him and she began right off trying to do things about him. It was Boyden's experience that it was always tough, at any rate for a man, to have a woman feel that she owned you. It was normal for a man to feel that way about a woman, but if a woman felt that way about a man it was a lot better if she did not show it.

That Christmas was in 1940, and they were always together after that, vacation times. Verna would go with him to see plays in New York, not musical shows but pretty deep stuff. If they were in town in the afternoons, instead of looking in the shop windows or going to a picture, she wanted to go to art galleries where you saw oil paintings of fallen-down barns and skulls of dead animals on the desert. She was different but it didn't gripe him. All that next year, his junior year, he would write her at Smith College where she went to school and she would send him books about China, and books of stories by men like Steinbeck. He read them whenever he had the time, because love was like that. Verna made him finish out his year when the war started instead of quitting cold the way a lot of the kids did. If it hadn't been for Verna May, he would have signed up that next Christmas after Pearl Harbor. She had cried when he had told her what he was going to do, instead of being proud of it, and it was uncomfortable having some kid cry on you when there was a war on. It was no time to be studying history and who socked Socrates when there was a war on, but he stuck it out till

April because they said you stood a better chance for a commission if you stayed in college. There wasn't any stopping him when it came April, and that was when Verna said something that upset him. She said it the afternoon when he got back from 90 Church Street, after the doctors had spent all day giving him the works.

"Jimmy, dear," Verna May said, "I wish you wouldn't act as though it were a football game."

Those were not the right words to use at a time like that, although it was his experience that most women were always emotionally unstable. Verna never seemed to understand that you had to pay your way for what had been given you and that if you didn't get in there and pitch a lot of little slant-eyed Joes would be kicking you around. She didn't seem to understand that anybody with guts wasn't going to sit around and let some college turn him into a quiz kid until his number was called.

"But, Jimmy," she said, "why do you have to go into aviation?"

She did not seem to understand that all the best kids were trying out for it; besides, it was better flying than walking in the mud; besides, you could get a commission and flying pay; and besides, it was something to aim at because it took guts; and besides, someone had to do it.

Yet this did not answer a part of Verna's question. What sort of faith did Boyden and those others like him have that made them brave? It must have been something more than the valor of sheer ignorance, and more than pride, or competition, or loyalty to a group. Somewhere there was some meaning in his meaninglessness that escaped all definition. They were dying every day for something.

Briggs was half asleep when he was aroused by someone shaking his shoulder. The pressure in his ears told him that the plane was letting down. The air was growing as sultry as July at home. They were letting down at Kwajalein and a weapon carrier would take them to the mess. Except for the airport and the kitchens, Kwajalein was sound asleep. He could see vaguely the outlines of barracks and supply depots and an occasional decapitated palm — the only visible monuments of the taking of the island. When the passengers trooped in and sat on the benches of the mess hall, it looked like an all-night diner. The lieutenant next him asked for the evaporated milk.

"It's a hot night," Briggs said.

"Yes," the lieutenant answered, "it really is hot. Are you going back to the States?" The lieutenant stirred his coffee and poured some syrup on his French toast. "The last time I was back I didn't know exactly what to say. Did you ever feel like that?"

"Yes," Briggs answered, "almost everybody does."

"It's like being two places at once when you're on leave," the lieutenant said.

He remembered that Boyden had said the same thing once. It was like adjusting two images in an optical instrument, but no matter what you did those two images would never exactly coincide.

V

BY THE TIME BOYDEN GOT
to Pensacola Verna May must have heard the other
girls talking because she seemed glad that he was in
there pitching. Somebody must have told her that
what the boys wanted most were good long letters
from home, because she wrote him letters that took
a long while to read, what with other things on your
mind. She told him how proud she was to have
someone who belonged to her — that's what she
said, "belonged to her" — fighting for his country,
and then she used to ask him what books he had
been reading. She would not have understood, if
he had told her that he used his spare time in other
ways. You saw a whole lot of the United States
when you were going to those different schools,
and you picked up a lot of new ideas. Somehow it
was hard for him always to keep Verna May in

his mind. He had her picture in his wallet and she had his at home, standing in front of the old crate he was learning to fly — but that did not mean he belonged to Verna May. He was definitely *not* engaged to her, although he and Verna may have talked the way you do sometimes about the future, but she should have known that he always did it in a kidding way, and besides there was a war on. He was getting too many new ideas to be able to read long letters, or to write many back. The truth was that he had not been in love with Verna May at all; he had simply in his mind made Verna May into the sort of girl he had wanted to love.

This was the sort of thing that crept up on you and smacked you, without your knowing it was coming. The truth was he could not blame himself for something that was an honest mistake. He had simply known Verna May before he had gone to all those flying schools. They shot a lot of stuff into you there that tended to make you different. You found yourself facing up to a lot of things that weren't the way they looked in print. You realized that you might die if you didn't remember what you were told, about reading a map, or manipulating gadgets. It didn't pay to have too much else on your mind, and yet in a way you noticed more things than you ever had, and sometimes after a hard day when something had almost happened to you but not quite, you were just very glad to be alive. Without its worrying you at all, you couldn't help but get, finally, into a new sort of mood.

He could not understand exactly why love should be mixed up in this mood, but it seemed to be that way with lots of people. Once he heard someone recite a poem. It was a kid in a sack near him who had a volume of Kipling, and the poem was about some things being greater than other things, and three of the things that were greater were women, and horses, and war. He did not know anything about horses, but maybe it was true about women.

Maybe love was different at different times according to your mood. At any rate down at Pensacola, not so long before he got his commission, he was at one of those Saturday night dances at the U.S.O., with no premonition that anything extraordinary would happen. He was simply down

there at the dance and someone had introduced
him to a little blonde who was quite a cute little
trick. She had a turned-up nose and blue eyes. She
said her people were sort of camping out in a
bungalow on Mariposa Avenue. She said that she
had been dancing with so many boys that her
feet hurt and she could not tell one from the other
and Boyden had asked her what she couldn't tell
apart — the boys or her feet. Later she said that
her feet hurt her so much, perhaps if he would take
her home, she could tell him apart from the other
boys. So he drove home with her in her car and
she took off her slippers, and then she took off
her stockings because it was a very hot night.

Her name was Daisy Sonberg. Her father had
lived in Charleston, West Virginia, before he had
retired, but he was really her stepfather, because
her mother had married again after a divorce and
she did not know where her father was and sometimes it made her sad and lonely. After a while
they began talking about life and they both agreed
that you could not tell what would happen next.
For instance, here they were just sitting alone on
the porch, although neither of them had known

the other existed the day before. Daisy was engaged to a boy who had left for Pearl, but now that she saw Boyden she was not sure whether she loved that boy or not, and Boyden told her he knew exactly what she meant because he suddenly realized he was in exactly the same situation. He was not at all sure that he was in love with Verna May. It was a very interesting thing to discuss, that lieutenant off at Pearl and Verna May in Orange. "We're just two lonely people, aren't we?" Daisy said.

It seemed that Daisy's stepfather and mother were off somewhere for the week end, so they had the bungalow all to themselves — just as though it were their own. When they went inside and Daisy got some ice and soda and a bottle of her stepfather's Bourbon — running out to the kitchen in her bare feet to fetch the glasses — it seemed to Boyden that he had always known Daisy. When they went around looking for the bottle opener and that gadget that pried the ice loose out of the tray, he realized the kid needed someone to help her, not like Verna May, who could always help herself. She cut her finger trying to open the soda bottle and then they had to look through the bathroom cabinet to find a band-aid for it. Then out in the kitchen she knocked over two glasses.

"You better park yourself on the sofa and let me handle this," Boyden said.

She looked up at him with her blue eyes wide open, just like a little kid, and she was shorter than he was — not taller like Verna May.

"I'm not fit to marry him," she said.

Of course she was referring to that unknown lieutenant out at Pearl, but Daisy was all right.

"You park yourself on the sofa," Boyden told her.

"My hair's a mess," she said, but he always liked her yellow hair when it was rumpled. It was just as though it were their own house when they sat on the sofa polishing off the Bourbon, and they had a pretty interesting and serious conversation. Just for one thing, they were both interested in that radio program where people told their problems once a week, and just the week before there had been a girl on that program who was engaged to one boy, but who had met a second one, and now could not tell which one she really loved.

The mediation board had said it was very coura-
geous of her to face the problem squarely, and that
if she kept on facing it, her instinct would tell her
which one she ought to marry.

"Listen, baby," Boyden said, "you don't love
that heel at Pearl."

"How do you know I don't?" Daisy asked.

"Because you wouldn't talk about him to me, if
you did," Boyden answered. That was when he
realized for certain that he had simply made Verna
May into the girl he wanted to love. Daisy sat on
the sofa, looking at her bare toes, with each little
toenail done with red nail paint, to match her
fingers.

"How do you make them match?" Boyden asked.

"They don't," Daisy said. "I lost the bottle I
did my hands with, and I couldn't remember the
color when I got one for my toes."

It was true when you looked. Her toes were one
color and her fingers were another.

"I wish I wasn't so mixed up," Daisy said, and
all at once she began to cry. It seemed that Daisy
hadn't been telling quite the truth about that boy
at Pearl. She hadn't wanted to because she was so

ashamed, but now that she knew Boyden better, she wanted to tell him that the boy had written, all of a sudden, and told her that it was all off.

It had not occurred to Boyden until a long while later that the kid at Pearl must have felt about Daisy just the way he was feeling about Verna May. Even when it did occur to him, he knew that there was no parallel, because Daisy was not Verna May.

"Darling," Daisy said, "I guess I'd better go to bed."

Boyden stood up, and picked up his cap.

"But where are you going to sleep?" Daisy asked him.

"I've got a twenty-four-hour pass," Boyden said. "I've got a sack at the hotel."

"You can sleep on the couch here, if you want," Daisy said, "the family won't be back until to-morrow night."

Now Verna May would never have had the courage to do that. She would have been afraid of what people would say. At any rate, it was a very romantic thing and Daisy did not care what people said. It was like living in a story — parts of it. Daisy's room was just off the parlor and while he lay there on the couch, they talked to each other through the half-open door. His nerves had never been so quiet. He had never slept so well; in fact he never woke up until nine the next morning, when he opened his eyes to find Daisy in a pink wrapper leaning over him. It was exactly as though it were their own house.

"Darling," Daisy said, "when I put the coffee on I broke the percolator."

There was nothing wrong about it and it was a very beautiful experience. It was quite a rest after all the technical stuff he had been learning, about astronomy and azimuths — something he could remember without its taking his mind off his work. The main thing that they wanted to be sure of was that they really loved each other as much as they thought they did, and the week after he was commissioned they knew they did. His pay was large enough to support a wife, particularly since he was going to sea, and so they were married two days later when he got his leave.

All the rest of it was like something which you thought about and which never seemed quite pos-

sible. He had bought an old jalopy there at Pensacola and he had a gas allotment to drive it north on
leave. Sometimes before Boyden went to sleep he
would think about that ride, and of all the places
where they had stopped along the coast — the pine
woods where the tire blew out, the night in the
tourist home in Savannah, the day in Charleston,
and the day in Washington. There was nothing
wrong with a single minute of it as far as he could
remember. Of course they were surprised at home
when they saw Daisy, but it was Boyden's experience that this sort of thing was happening all the
time, now that there was a war on. Although thirty
days was not much, it was time enough to get
things squared away. Daisy was not very good at
looking out for herself and he wanted her to be in
an apartment in East Orange where she could be
comfortable and secure, right with his own people
in case she was going to have a baby or anything
like that. Sometimes when he thought of luck he
thought of himself and Daisy. It had been good
luck that they had found the apartment on Maple
Street, exactly the right size. It had been good
luck after that leave was over that they had been

able to travel together, in a lower berth, out to the West Coast and find two rooms at San Diego.

You got to know someone very well, particularly a girl like Daisy, when you batted around here and there the way you did in this war. You got to know what love was, living in little shacks and one-night stands on the West Coast while you were waiting for your orders. But the best part of it was that there were all sorts of married kids from all over the country in just the same position, so that you made a lot of friends and had a swell time while you were waiting for your orders. Everybody was kind to you, even the brass. His squadron commander had them to dinner twice, right at his apartment in San Francisco, just as though they were the same age. It was a great experience being married to anyone like Daisy, and that wasn't like anybody else's experience. It was something to know that all you had to do when you got leave was to send a wire when you reached the Coast. It was something to remember that she was right there, with a kid fifteen months old that he had never seen, but he had the pictures and the letters. It was something to remember.

"It's kind of funny," Boyden said, "having a kid in just that way."

"In just what way?" Briggs asked him.

Boyden shook his head when he tried to think of the right answer.

"In that way," Boyden said; "all ready-made."

"It's the fashion now," Briggs said.

"Without doing anything about it," Boyden said; "that is, at least, not very much. All ready-made. It's hard to believe, isn't it?"

"You'll believe it when you see him," Briggs said.

"Yes, I suppose so, when I see him," Boyden said. "You're married, aren't you, Pop? Did you ever get so you didn't remember exactly how it happened?"

"You mean, so much else has been happening?" Briggs asked him.

"Yes," Boyden said, "maybe. You have to work quick when there's a war on. Sometimes I look at the pictures and I can't remember. Sometimes it's like it's all ready-made without my making it. That's what I mean when I say I don't remember."

There was the story of Lieutenant Boyden, a

sequence of a few natural impulses and a few automatic responses. Yet the character that produced those impulses and responses was capable of others. With that unpromising background for a beginning, Lieutenant James K. Boyden could wear, if he wanted to wear ribbons, the Ribbon of the Navy Cross, the Distinguished Flying Cross and the Aid Medal with a Gold Star. If he still thought about the war as an athletic event, he was winning all the cups. . . .

The lieutenant next to Briggs nudged him. "Johnston," he said, and Briggs turned to look through the small round window behind him.

"Remember the sign in the head at Johnston?" the lieutenant asked, "about going easy on the water? One gallon of fuel oil to distill one gallon of drinking water, or is it two gallons?"

It was dawn, and the cloud formations were a soft pink above the pastel blue of the ocean. Johnston Island lay below them, a man-made airstrip built upon a shoal, and Briggs could see the half circle of breakers on the coral reef. It looked incredibly remote and small, and the faint colors of dawn made it weird and beautiful. Screwball islands, Boyden had called the Pacific atolls once — bodies of water completely surrounded by land, and no wonder too many screwy sights like that drove some kids nuts. . . . Full fathom five . . . The pink clouds, the half light in the plane, the strained unshaven faces of the passengers, and then some slight change in the revolution of the motors must have brought the words to Briggs's memory . . . Full fathom five . . . and too many of those screwy islands drove some kids nuts. The rest of the words came back to him, fantastic restive words, a half answer to everything he had been thinking. They were all sunk fathoms deep in the unnatural element of war. No one who had ever been out there would ever be the same again.

> Full fathom five thy father lies;
> Of his bones are coral made;
> Those are pearls that were his eyes:
> Nothing of him that doth fade
> But doth suffer a sea-change
> Into something rich and strange.
> Sea-nymphs hourly ring his knell . . .

VI

IT WAS SNOWING IN NEW York and the snow and an undercurrent of sound half blotted out the city the afternoon that William Briggs took the bus to Orange. The bus was crowded and the air inside was thick and wet and damp. He had never been a commuter and he felt awkward and out of place. He had tried several times to get in touch with Daisy, though he had a good many problems of his own. It was hard enough getting accustomed again to his own friends. There was an atmosphere of unreality about the old faces, and about his former habits, and association had no permanence because he was going out again. When he called the number which Boyden had given him, he was told several times that it did not answer; then he was told that the number was out of order and finally that it had been discontinued. He sent two telegrams also, but there was no reply. At length on a Saturday morning he was able to reach Boyden's family, and Boyden's father was at home. That was when he learned that Daisy was away for a few days, but was expected back that evening, and wouldn't he come out for supper?

"Hello, Mr. Boyden?" he said. "My name is Briggs, William Briggs. I am just back from the Pacific where I saw your son, Jimmy."

"What's that?" Mr. Boyden asked. From his voice it might have been Lieutenant Boyden speaking. "You say you've just seen Jimmy?"

"Yes," Briggs answered. "He wanted me to tell you he's doing fine."

Of course he would come out. It would not be any trouble. It would be a pleasure, the least that he could do. Orange was only a step from New York and he would be glad to stay for supper. Boysie — that is, Jimmy; they called him Boysie out there on the carrier — had told him so much about his family that he felt he knew them already.

That was the way one always put it. He couldn't go back without having seen them, and if they had

any messages — yes, he was going back again —
it would be no trouble at all. It would be a pleasure,
the least that anyone could do. That was the way
one always put it — the least, and it was almost nothing. He knew that if he had not gone it would have
been like leaving the theater before the last cur-
tain. There was something along that bus-line for
which someone like Boyden cared to die.

As the bus moved through the Oranges, starting
and stopping in the snow and dusk, Briggs could
not escape the feeling that he was visiting an important place — the dwelling of some great man,
with its furnishings still preserved intact. It was
like a charabanc trip to some region in England,
to some tourists' literary shrine — a trip through
the Holland Tunnel to the Boyden country, in-
cluding a visit to the boyhood home of James K.
Boyden.

He knew the house without looking for the
number. He could tell it by the porch and by the
pitch of the roof, and by the lines which were
already a little dated. He could almost believe that
Boyden was watching him, telling him that it was
not that house or that one, but the one with the

yellow paint and with the maple tree in front of it — the one with the service star and the Red Cross sticker in the window.

Mr. Boyden was frail, with mouse-gray hair, but he was easy to recognize because his lips curled up like Boyden's when he smiled. He was dressed in a newly pressed blue serge suit which Briggs imagined had been kept for particular occasions.

"It's kind of you to come on a night like this," Mr. Boyden said. "I hope you didn't slip on the front steps."

"Oh, no," Briggs answered, "it's nice to see some snow."

"Let me take your coat," Mr. Boyden said, "and just go right into the parlor. I'll tell them that you've come."

While Briggs stood in the parlor waiting, he could hear Mr. Boyden cross the hall and open the kitchen door. It was obvious that he would have broccoli for supper.

"Carrie," he heard Mr. Boyden say, "I guess the bus was early."

"Well, entertain him for just a minute, Philip. We'll be right out," he heard Mrs. Boyden say, "and Philip?"

"Yes, Carrie."

"Did you get that bottle from the package store?"

"Yes, Carrie."

"Well, use the tall glasses — not those, the other ones."

The overstuffed parlor suite, the antimacassars, the radio with the Jacobean legs and the upright piano, and the golden oak bookcase with the set of Conrad were so exactly what they should have been that the room in which Briggs stood, and all its furnishings, seemed like a projection of his own imaginative efforts. Now all these homely objects served the single purpose of drawing the eye to a silver-framed photograph that stood upon a small lace-covered table.

It was, of course, a picture of Boyden, standing full length in Navy khaki, wearing all his decorations. It had obviously been done by a Honolulu photographer who had no time for nuances; in fact, you could almost hear the photographer saying: —

"Stand there, Buddy, and hold it. There's a long line waiting. Now, come and get it tomorrow morning. . . . Five dollars' deposit, please."

The lighting was pitiless, but the effect was

amazingly lifelike. You could see from his round eyes that Boyden did not want to have the damned thing taken and that he must have given his hair a quick shove from his forehead an instant before the shutter clicked, for his right hand was still in mid-air with its fingers half opened. Briggs was sure that Boyden had been about to speak. Words seemed to come from his half-parted lips.

You could almost hear him saying, "Get on with it, Pops, I'm busy myself."

When Mr. Boyden returned, Briggs was still looking at the photograph. "There's Jimmy. It's a speaking likeness, isn't it?" Mr. Boyden said. He was carrying a black tray with lace over it. There was a pink bowl on the tray filled with ice cubes, and two glasses, one bottle of whiskey and one of soda. "Jimmy often wrote about you." . . . Mr. Boyden raised his glass and looked at it uncertainly. "He said he talked to you a lot."

Briggs laughed.

"He used to call me Pops."

"Jimmy always had fresh names for everybody," Mr. Boyden said.

"He gave me a message to give you," Briggs

said. "He wanted me to tell you that you're a damned good guy. Those are his words, not mine."

"Thanks," Mr. Boyden said, and his voice broke. "Excuse me, well — yes — Jimmy's a good boy."

"I hope I'll be seeing him before long," Briggs said. "He'll want to hear about everything — particularly about Daisy."

There was silence and then Mr. Boyden cleared his throat.

"Oh, yes, Daisy. She'll be back tonight," he said. "She left the baby with us. It's easier having grandchildren."

"All the fun and none of the worry," Briggs said.

"What's that?" Mr. Boyden asked. "Oh, yes, not nearly so much worry. I wish you'd tell me something — before the women come."

He stopped and a sharp sizzling sound came from the oven of the automatic stove in the kitchen.

"Roast lamb," Mr. Boyden said. "I wish you'd tell me before they come. Did you get the impression that anything was worrying Jimmy?"

Briggs laughed uneasily. "Not Jimmy. He isn't the worrying kind," he said.

"It was only that he said that he talked to you a

lot." Mr. Boyden's eyes were on the picture. "Jimmy used to talk when he was worried. Well, here they are — " Mr. Boyden smiled. "This is Mrs. Boyden, Mr. Briggs, and here's my daughter, Susie," and then he added for no apparent reason, "Jimmy's sister. Now you know all the family."

Briggs believed that motherhood had become more of a cult than ever since the beginning of the war. For some reason it was generally admitted that mothers suffered more than fathers. It seemed to Briggs that Mrs. Boyden was just the sort of person who would never forget that she was an American mother, with an American son at the front. She was plump and deep-bosomed with graying auburn hair tied in a hard knot. Her face was round like Boyden's and she wore pince-nez glasses, and a service pin on her purple satin afternoon dress. She would never be able to understand what her son was going through but she would be very brave. It was obvious that she wanted Briggs to feel that she had only been out in the kitchen for just a minute and that she did her own housework only because she liked to have things nice.

"I hope you're not starving, Mr. Briggs," she

said, "and please excuse our scurrying back and forth. It's so much easier not having a maid."

"Yes," Susie said, "there's no one to get mad and leave when we're late."

He had seen Susie's picture with all of Boyden's others, but somehow he had not realized that Susie would be short and chunky, too, like Boyden, with Boyden's sandy eyebrows and his straight, even teeth.

"I told Philip not to ask you any questions before I came, because everyone wants to hear everything," Mrs. Boyden said. "It's such a small world, isn't it? And to have a real live war correspondent in the house."

Susie giggled.

"He had to be alive to get here, didn't he?"

"Philip," Mrs. Boyden crooked her finger at Mr. Boyden, "did you forget to close the furnace?"

"No, dear," Mr. Boyden answered.

Mrs. Boyden seated herself and smoothed her satin skirt and adjusted her service pin.

"Now," she said, "let's begin at the beginning. When did you first meet Jimmy, Mr. Briggs?"

It was what he had come to tell them, but he was

wondering as he started to speak how the elder Boydens must have looked when they were younger. They were asking him to begin at the beginning, when they were the beginning.

"Well," Briggs began, "the first time I saw Jimmy was quite a while ago at Pearl Harbor after he had been picked up from a raft, but of course you know all about it."

"You really saw him then? We have all the clippings in Jimmy's scrapbook," Mrs. Boyden said. "The newspapers reported it beautifully."

"It was just by accident that I got to know him," Briggs went on. "We were staying at the same hotel and Jimmy asked me up to his room and told me a lot about the war."

"I bet he was drinking," Susie said.

Mrs. Boyden looked hurt. "No one in Jimmy's position would dream of doing anything like that, especially when he had just been given the Navy Cross, would he, Mr. Briggs?"

"Well, as a matter of fact," Briggs said, "you know the flight surgeons themselves recommend that the fliers take a little something now and then."

He stopped. The doorbell was ringing, and with the sound everything in the room had stopped. Mrs. Boyden drew a sharp breath.

"It's only Verna May and Sam," Susie said quickly. "Don't you remember that you asked them over? Don't worry, Mom."

"Oh, yes," Mrs. Boyden said and her face lighted up again. "Verna May, that is, Miss Lewis, is a childhood friend of Jimmy's, Mr. Briggs, and her fiancé, Sergeant Tilton, was one of Jimmy's old friends, too. . . . I always think it may be a telegram."

"Oh, yes," Briggs said, "I've heard of Verna May, but I hadn't heard — "

"It hasn't been announced yet," Mrs. Boyden said hastily.

He was shaking hands with Verna May and he remembered that Boyden had called her a cute little trick, but it was not a good description. She was the sort of girl that a mother would want her son to marry — a tall reliable girl, with a clear complexion, nice hands and straight shoulders. Her cheeks were red from the cold. Her nose was thin and so was her mouth.

"I hope we haven't missed anything," said Verna May.

"Oh, not a thing, dear," Mrs. Boyden said, "and may I present Sam, that is, Sergeant Tilton."

Then he was shaking hands with Sam Tilton who had taught Boyden so much about women. Sam was a technical sergeant in a tailor-made uniform. His eyes, behind metal-framed glasses, were limpid brown. He had slick hair, and a quick easy smile.

"Sam," Mr. Boyden said, "how about a little Scotch?"

"Oh, no," Verna May said. "Not anything for Sam."

"Thanks, just the same," Sam said hoarsely. "I'm sort of off it, Mr. Boyden."

"Carrie," Mr. Boyden cleared his throat again, "don't you think we ought to call up Daisy?"

Briggs was aware of the same sort of silence that had fallen on the room when the bell had rung.

"Philip," Mrs. Boyden said, "we've been all over that."

Then Briggs remembered Boyden's souvenirs. They were wrapped in a brown paper package, and everyone watched him slip off the string and open it, as though he were performing a conjuring trick.

The souvenirs were the sort that anyone might pick up on a battlefield — a Japanese soldier's diary which should have been given to the Intelligence, a pile of Japanese bills, a canteen, a revolver, a clock from a Japanese plane, and a silk battle flag.

"You don't think they have disease germs?" Mrs. Boyden asked.

"I choose the flag," called Susie.

"Silly — that's for Daisy, of course," said Verna May. "You'll get me a flag, too, won't you, Sam, when you go to the Pacific?"

"Sure," Sam said, "right off Hirohito, Verna."

The dining room told its own mute story of unmitigated effort. There was a tablecloth of Italian lace that could not have been used for years, as Briggs could tell from the slight discoloration at the folds. There was a mirror centerpiece, with two glass swans and an agate goldfish upon it, all swimming toward a cut-glass bowl filled with snapdragons and ferns. The place plates were the color of Paris green and on each plate were figures of foxhunters in pink coats. There were heavy tumblers of handcut glass, and pinkish-purple wineglasses, and lace-edged napkins each with a little piece of bread inside it. There were butter plates and small plates of salad, each containing four grapefruit sections, a single leaf of lettuce, one prune stuffed with cream cheese, one red and one green Maraschino cherry and a dab of mayonnaise. There were also place cards, decorated with bluebirds, for each of the six guests.

Briggs pulled out Mrs. Boyden's chair, and then they waited while the two girls brought in yellow bouillon cups of clear consommé from the kitchen.

"I'm going to ask Mr. Briggs to say the blessing," Mrs. Boyden said.

Briggs recalled what Boyden had said about the Altar Guild, and his thoughts moved desperately to memories of the last church supper he had attended, but he could not recollect the words of any grace. The last religious words he had heard were from the service of a burial at sea. For an instant he could see the crew detail with their rifles, the chaplain in his robes with his Book of Common Prayer, and the body on the grating underneath the flag.

"O Lord," he began, and stopped. His voice was hoarse and the palms of his hands were moist. "O Lord, bless this food for thy servants' use, Amen."

He was not sure that it was adequate but it was near enough. His hand groped for a round bouillon spoon.

"You might pass the claret, Philip," Mrs. Boyden said. "I see you looking at the swans, Mr. Briggs. Jimmy gave them to me for Christmas once. He knew that I like to have things nice."

"Oh," Verna May said. "Why, I was with Jimmy when he bought them. We knew that you liked crystal."

"No thanks, Mr. Boyden," Briggs heard Sam Tilton say. "I'm kind of off wine."

"Sam's in Division Headquarters now," Verna May told them. "He's in charge of all the mimeographing."

Mrs. Boyden picked up her bouillon spoon and smiled at Briggs. "You mustn't mind if the girls pop up and down, but please tell us all about Jimmy."

When Briggs began he knew he would be fitting

everything he told into terms of the Boydens' dining room — minimizing the danger, making it all sound comfortable and reassuring.

It was a beautiful sight to see the planes take off and circle above the ship. Jimmy was a fine pilot. The thing to remember was that the Japanese fleet was no longer the menace that it used to be. He was aware of the lamb with browned potatoes and brown gravy, and mint jelly and broccoli and Hollandaise, and vanilla ice cream and chocolate sauce and lady fingers. Life on a carrier was not always exciting. A lot of the time it was like a southern cruise, with the boys in shorts taking sunbaths. There was plenty of clean linen, a fine free laundry, and moving pictures, and the food right here was almost but not quite as good as the carrier food. They had their own ice cream machine.

True, there were moments of excitement, especially when a task force was near the Japanese Islands. There were occasional plane attacks and there were, just as you read in the papers, the Divine Wind planes, or the "One-way Boys," as they were sometimes called, but the thing to remember was that these attacks were all over in a matter of seconds.

"Not nearly as bad as you might think," he heard himself saying. There was always the air cover and the radar always picked them up. And the *Rogue River* was a lucky ship. Briggs knew that he was doing well. He was telling them what they wanted most to hear.

"My main impression on the *Rogue River*," he was saying, "was of everyone's being friendly and having a good time." Maybe they didn't know what a hand Jimmy was at bridge. And maybe they didn't know how good he was at card tricks and sleight-of-hand. He was the life of the party there on the *Rogue River*.

"Girls," Mrs. Boyden said, "I think it might be nice to have our demitasses in the parlor, but don't stop talking, Mr. Briggs."

When they were back in the parlor, Mr. Boyden gave him a cigar in a cellophane wrapper, and Briggs finished it while he went on talking. He was trying to think of amusing anecdotes. It was amusing to hear the boys talking over the interphones when the squadron was in the air. You could hear

the air fights sometimes right there on the island —
the superstructure of the ship, not a real island. Of
course, planes were forced down at sea occasionally
as Jimmy's had been that time off Formosa, but
you would be amazed at the high percentage of
rescues.

"They have it down to a system," he heard himself saying, "and the system's getting better all
the time."

When he had finished his cigar he rose and said
that he was afraid he had been talking too much
and that he really had to be going. He wondered
if they could tell him where Maple Street was.
Jimmy would never forgive him if he did not call
at Maple Street.

"Of course," Mrs. Boyden said. "It's been very
selfish of us. We couldn't get Daisy for supper, you
know, but I'm sure she'll be back by now. We
might send Daisy some ice cream, don't you think
so, Philip?"

"What's that?" Mr. Boyden asked. "Oh, yes, of
course he must see Daisy. He can see her and get
the eleven o'clock bus. I'll walk to the corner
with him."

Then Mrs. Boyden thought of something else. She must have thought of it while Verna May was saying how wonderful it had been just to sit and listen.

"It certainly was great," Sam Tilton was telling him, "to hear all that about old Jimmy, right from the horse's mouth."

"Why, we've forgotten the most important thing," Mrs. Boyden cried. "We've forgotten all about Baby."

"Oh," Verna May said, "hasn't he seen him?"

"We can all go up," Mrs. Boyden said. "I'll lead the way and you follow me, Mr. Briggs, and you'll excuse it if things are a little higgledy-piggledy upstairs — you know how things are with a baby."

Everyone walked into the hall and began moving up the narrow stairs in single file.

"You see, Daisy leaves him with us sometimes," Mrs. Boyden whispered. "She knows we love it so and she forgets formulas sometimes. She says herself she's not very good with babies."

The narrow hall upstairs was lit by a dim electric light and had that odor which one associates with extreme youth.

"You must tell Jimmy that you saw him in Jimmy's own bedroom," Mrs. Boyden whispered. "It's almost like having Jimmy all over, all the fun and none of the bother."

The door squeaked faintly as Mrs. Boyden opened it and stepped into the dark. She switched on a shaded light, and Briggs followed her into the little room where Boyden used to sleep. He could see the picture of the high school class and the fraternity in the faint light, and a banner on the wall with the numerals of Boyden's college class. He could see Boyden's bureau with a pair of military brushes on it. The baby was sleeping in a basket in Boyden's narrow bed, and beside the bed was a combination bathtub and changing table, and a pile of diapers and a bottle warmer.

"Hush," Mrs. Boyden whispered. "He looks just the way Jimmykins looked — not like his mama at all."

But all that Briggs could see was a round and pasty baby with arms thrown upward and fists clenched, pale, as infants always were when they were sound asleep, exuding a faint odor of sour milk.

"Susie," Mrs. Boyden whispered. "Don't forget to take him up in half an hour."

Outside it had stopped snowing and the air was clear as it always was after snow.

"This ought to be the last snowstorm," Mr. Boyden said. "There's been a lot of snow this winter."

They stopped under a street lamp at the corner and Mr. Boyden thrust his hands into his overcoat pockets.

"You see . . ." he said, and he hesitated and began again. "I wish Mrs. Boyden and Susie got on better with Jim's wife, not that you need tell him, but you know how women are . . . a little jealous, sometimes. I suppose you must have noticed, or I wouldn't have brought it up."

Briggs did not know what to answer.

"It's the strain," Mr. Boyden added. "You saw . . . when the doorbell rang. It's harder for women."

Neither of them moved, and Mr. Boyden spoke again.

"I can't thank you enough for telling us so much."

"It was a pleasure," Briggs said, "the least I could do."

"Two blocks down and to the left," Mr. Boyden said; "the only stucco house. It's the downstairs apartment to the right, and the bus leaves at eleven o'clock in front of the filling station, but Daisy can take you down. Thanks again for everything, Mr. Briggs."

VII

"IT'S THE THIRD HOUSE down on Maple Street, the only double stucco house, and remember there's a goddam funny tree in front of it — the only one like it there."

The street lights made luminous circles on the fresh snow, which were cut by the shadows of bare branches of maple trees. The gabled houses on their small white lawns were cold and dark, for it was getting late on Maple Street. The only stucco house was a three-story building, geometrical and solid, the kind that contractors had once erected hastily for investment purposes. The tree in front, as Briggs had guessed already, was an umbrella tree, with a bare network of little branches reaching down to the snow.

The lower right-hand mail box bore the name of Boyden in sprawling block letters, so there was no doubt that it was the apartment where the kid was waiting safe and sound. It was a quarter of ten o'clock, a little late to drop in suddenly, but Briggs could see lights behind the drawn shades of the downstairs windows. He thought that there would be a pause when he rang the outer bell, but instead the electric latch began to click before he had finished ringing.

"Don't slam the front door, darling. Don't wake everybody up."

He heard Daisy whisper before he even saw her, but when he was in the hall she gave a little gasp.

"Oh, my God," Daisy said. "I thought it was someone else." She stood with the light of the room behind her, so that he could only judge the expression on her face by her voice, but he remembered hearing Boyden say that Daisy always did too much at once.

"I'm sorry," Briggs was still speaking to the shadow of Daisy in the apartment door. "My name is Briggs. I'm a friend of Jimmy's. I'm just back from the Pacific. He said he'd written about me. I hope he did."

"Oh, yes," she said. "Oh, yes, that's so. Well, come on in."

The place reminded him of the hotel room where he had first talked with Lieutenant Boyden. It had exactly the same sort of disorder, and the same perfunctory decoration. The walls and the woodwork were cream color and the floor was varnished golden oak, partially covered by a factory-made hooked rug, decorated by a profusion of green leaves and purple flowers that clashed with the ready-made "drapes" at the windows. Stockings and underwear bulged from an open suitcase. Some other stockings were in one corner of a sofa, and a coat and a tiny hat were in the other corner. Gingerale bottles and groceries and unwashed dishes and glasses were heaped on chairs and tables.

"I am sorry," Briggs said, "I shouldn't have dropped in like this."

"Oh, that's all right," Daisy said. "It's swell that you stopped in."

She held out a thin little hand with dark red pointed fingernails, and Briggs remembered what Boyden had said about her fingers and her toes that night at Pensacola. She was smiling at him, and her blonde hair, very soft and undulating from a permanent, fell rumpled to her shoulders.

Briggs stood there under the glare of the unshaded ceiling fixture, comparing a photograph with its subject, for of course he had seen her picture with Boyden's other pictures. She looked even younger than he had imagined, too young to be worried about marriage or a baby, too young to keep the room neat, or to worry about the facts of life.

She looked like those glamor girls in the movie magazines, like Betty Grable or Veronica Lake, snapped informally at home, although you knew, if you had any sense, that their poses were far from informal. She had the same beguiling stare, the same half-parted lips just about to break into a smile, the same narrowing of the corners of the eyes. He could imagine that she was pretending she was not Daisy Boyden at all, but Lana Turner receiving an inquiring photographer. He could imagine her preparing to say that she loved simple, outdoor sports and babies.

"Gee," Daisy Boyden said. "I wish I'd known you were coming, and I'd have put something on."

Her eyebrows were plucked to pencil lines and a wide bow of lipstick had given her one of those disdainful artificial mouths which he had noticed were the latest fashion. She was wearing a pink silk negligee wrapped over blue pajamas. It might have been the same negligee that Daisy had worn at Pensacola on that romantic night — a little worn and spotted, but very, very pretty.

"You look very nice," Briggs said.

"Gee," she said, "well, thanks a lot! I didn't mean to be so informal, but I can take it if you can."

"I could come back again," Briggs said, "if you're expecting someone."

"Oh that's all right," Daisy said, "he's just a friend — that is, kind of. Boysie wrote me all about you, but I didn't know it would be like this."

Briggs did not know that it would be either and, furthermore, he still did not know just what it was like.

" 'Boysie,' " Briggs said. "That's what they called him on the carrier. I didn't know you called him that."

"Me? I made it up, and the other kids must have heard me when we were running around together,"

Daisy answered. "A name kind of goes with someone — 'Boysie.' Things happen in funny ways,
don't they, in this life?"

"What sort of things?" Briggs asked.

"Oh, everything," Daisy said. "You knowing
Boysie, and then seeing me like this. I don't see
you getting on with Boysie exactly, but then life
is a sort of a rat-race, isn't it?"

"Yes, if you want to put it that way," Briggs
said. It was exactly the way to put it, considering
Daisy and the room.

"Everybody keeps coming and going," Daisy
said. "You are going back out there again, aren't
you?"

"Yes, in a few weeks," Briggs answered. "Boysie
will want to hear all about you when I see him."

"Well, that's just swell you're going back!" Daisy
said, and she pulled her silk wrap tighter about her
narrow shoulders. "It makes everything just swell.
Just throw your hat and coat down anywhere. I
guess you're used to layouts like this if you've
been around with the Navy."

"I've been trying to get in touch with you,"
Briggs said, "but I hear you've been away."

"Yes, down to Atlantic City." Daisy took a fresh package of cigarettes from a carton on the floor and tapped it with her thin fingers. "Gosh, it really is a marathon down there. I guess you've been seeing Boysie's people if you heard I was away."

"Yes," Briggs answered. "I was there for dinner."

"Oh, boy," Daisy said, and she lighted a cigarette. "I guess you need a drink, Pops. You don't mind if I call you Pops? . . . There's a bottle in the kitchen and some soda, if we can find an opener."

The heels of her soiled pink mules clicked like castanets as he followed her down a bare passage. He had a glimpse of a bedroom with dresses piled on an unmade studio couch, and the kitchenette was littered with pots and pans, empty cans, and baby's bottles.

"Did you see the kid?" she asked.

"Yes," he answered, "I saw the kid."

"He's a cute little number, isn't he? Here's the rye." Daisy held the bottle up and shook it.

"Boysie sent you a Japanese flag," Briggs said.

"Oh," Daisy said, "wasn't that angelic of Boysie?"

He had never known anyone like her, but he was beginning to understand what Boyden meant when he had said she was a cute little trick. She had so little to conceal. If he had been Boyden's age, he might also have started talking to her about life and love.

"Gosh, but things move fast. Do they ever get you all mixed up?" Daisy asked. Her sleeve caught on the handle of a saucepan and it clattered to the floor.

"Yes," Briggs answered, "sometimes."

"Just throw the coat and hat over on the floor," Daisy said when they were back in the living room. "Sometimes it makes me dizzy the way things happen. Sometimes, I don't know where I am after being around so much. It's funny, being in love."

"The thing to remember," Briggs said, and he was beginning to see what it must have been like at Pensacola, "is that everybody's been in the same boat sometime."

Daisy sat down on a corner of the sofa, and curled her legs under her.

"I guess we'd better have a little talk about

Boysie," she said. "Maybe you can see — I need someone who can see what I'm going through. Boysie used to say I did too many things at once. You can't help what life makes you, can you?"

"No, of course you can't," Briggs answered gently. "But you must not let it bother you. It ought to help to remember that Boysie's very fond of you. He thinks of you a lot."

At first he thought she had not heard him. She looked straight ahead of her at nothing, and clasped and unclasped her hands.

"I know. He thinks of me the way I used to be, but you can't stay still." She stopped and sighed. "Oh, boy, he used to be a sweet kid. I guess I've got to have someone around loving me the way he did. Some girls are made that way."

Yes, Briggs thought, some girls were made that way. All at once her voice had a tinkling ringing quality like the sound that came when you tapped the edge of a delicate glass and if you tapped the glass too hard it would break.

"Listen," Briggs said uneasily, "I know it's hard when someone you love is away." He had never intended to be plunged into Daisy's private life, and he hoped that if he did not look at her he might somehow avoid it.

She had turned toward him slowly, and he was afraid that she was going to cry. "If we could have only always been around together . . . We had the sweetest time. When Boysie left me here, Oh God . . . it was awful."

"Now, wait a minute," Briggs said hastily, "it will be all right when he comes back."

"No, it won't," he heard her say. "I don't love him any more . . . but I tried. I wish you'd tell him that. I really tried."

Boyden was right. When there was a war on you shouldn't get to liking anyone too much.

"Of course you love him," Briggs said. "Listen, you can't do that to him, not when he's where he is. You've got to love him."

"It doesn't matter where he is, you can't go on loving someone if you're not in love," she said.

"But I'm telling you," Briggs answered, "you don't know whether you love him or not because he isn't here."

Daisy shook her head. "It doesn't do any good to argue. You can't help what happens in this life.

I don't love Boysie any more. I'm engaged to someone else."

"You're what?" Briggs asked.

"I'm engaged to someone else — to the man I
was engaged to before I saw Jimmy."

"Now, wait a minute," Briggs began, "you can't
be engaged to one boy when you're married to
another."

"Oh, yes, I can," Daisy said, "a lot of girls are
now. I wish you'd see." Her voice was higher and
she was speaking slowly, as though she were ex-
asperated by his dullness. "*Someone's got* to explain
it to Boysie. I've thought and thought about it and
my idea is — you don't know what is going to happen to you when you get married — nobody does.
I thought I was in love with Boysie, but I really
wasn't. Boysie thought he was in love with someone else and he really wasn't."

"If it's all the same with you," Briggs said, "can't
you stop talking about love?" But Daisy was not
listening.

"You can't tell what's going to happen when you
get married. I couldn't know what being married
to Boysie was like until I tried it, could I? . . .

and I didn't know what it would be like having a baby either."

"People do have babies when they're married," Briggs began.

"But you can't tell what it's like until you have one," Daisy said. "Anyway, they'll take care of him . . . and I didn't know how it would be when Hugh came back."

"Who's Hugh?" Briggs asked; "the other boy?"

"Yes," Daisy said. "You'll like him when you see him. He's a good deal like Boysie only more so. That's what fooled me — only . . ."

"Only, what?" Briggs asked.

"I don't know," Daisy said. "Just only. You can't tell what's going to happen when you get married in a war."

"That's true," Briggs said. "I suppose it is the war."

The corners of Daisy's eyes wrinkled and she smiled.

"That's sweet of you to say that," she said. "I knew you'd see. And you can see that I've got to marry Hugh, can't you, and you can make Boysie see?"

There was no use telling her what he thought of her, and he was no longer sure what he thought, and certainly he was never meant to be a Voice of Experience, or an Old Friend of the Family.

"Do you mean to say," Briggs asked, "that you expect me to tell all this to Boysie?"

"I think it would be kinder, don't you," Daisy said, "than writing to him and asking right out for a divorce?"

"But can't you wait until he gets back on leave again?" Briggs asked. "You're the one who ought to tell him."

"It would be nicer," Daisy said, "but you see I can't wait very well. You see, I think — something must have gone wrong somewhere — I think I'm going to have another baby."

Briggs glanced helplessly about the room and its disorder was just like Daisy's mind. He rose and picked up his overcoat.

"I don't know why," he began, "I should be dragged into this mess — " but a buzzing sound in the kitchen stopped him, and Daisy was on her feet, the heels of her mules clattering as she ran.

"Here's Hugh," she said.

He had read about this sort of thing in social workers' notes. Mrs. B, naval officer's wife, unstable background; rudimentary education; emotionally immature; unable to adapt herself to new environment; has child, quarrels with husband's family; has now formed connection with other naval officer; believes is about to have child by this man . . .

Those facts would not have surprised him if he had read them on a file card. He would have said it was war psychosis and let it go at that, but it was not the same when he sat there and observed it.

"Don't slam the front door, darling," Daisy whispered. She led a naval lieutenant, the one she really loved, into the room, and closed the door.

"Hey," the officer said. "Who's the company?" and Daisy introduced them — this was Hugh Kroll, and this was that war correspondent who knew Boysie.

"And he's being awfully sweet and understanding about our problem, darling," Daisy said.

"Well, thanks a lot, sir," said Lieutenant Kroll, "but there isn't much to understand, is there?"

She had said that Lieutenant Kroll was like Boysie, only more so. Lieutenant Kroll's face was longer than Boyden's and whiter, and his hair was darker. It was the sort of face that is sometimes called a frank, open countenance.

"Well," Briggs said, "I think I'll be going now."

"Oh — not *now*," Daisy said, "when Hugh's just come. Besides you haven't heard it all."

"I've heard enough," Briggs said, "to get a pretty good picture. It won't be any use to hear much more."

"But you're going to help us," she told him. "You said you were — about the divorce."

He had not intended to pass any moral comment, or to show the way he felt, but suddenly his distaste for the whole shabby picture and his respect for Boyden's homely and fundamental virtues overcame sensible restraint.

"I never promised anything of the sort," he said, "but now that your friend is here," he turned away from her and looked straight at Lieutenant Kroll, "I'd like to ask him a question. I see you've served in the Pacific — you've been in action, haven't you, Lieutenant Kroll?"

"That's right, sir," Lieutenant Kroll said, "mostly with the LSTs."

"Don't call him 'sir,' Hugh," Daisy said, "he's nice."

He wished the girl would stop talking. He wanted to tell her that the whole thing was her fault and that she never should have been born.

"Listen, son," Briggs said. "How do you feel about taking another man's wife behind his back?"

Briggs had not raised his voice but he could feel his anger rising, and he felt a savage satisfaction when he saw the lieutenant's face grow red.

"How do I feel?" the lieutenant repeated.

"Yes," Briggs answered. "That's what I asked you."

The lieutenant hesitated a moment.

"You're giving me hard words, sir," he said. "You're being pretty rugged."

"Not very," Briggs said. "I'm simply curious. You don't have to answer if you don't want to."

Briggs put on his hat and began getting into his overcoat.

"Oh, I'll answer all right," the lieutenant said. "I'll tell you how I feel. I feel it's all fair and it squares up."

"Oh, do you?" Briggs asked.

"All fair," the lieutenant repeated. "That guy she's married to took her away from me when I was out at Pearl."

"But I thought you'd thrown her over," Briggs said.

"Who said I'd thrown her over?" Lieutenant Kroll asked.

"Why, whoever made such a lousy crack as that?" Daisy said before Briggs could answer. Her china-blue eyes were wide and innocent.

Briggs gazed at her uncertainly. He felt sorry for Lieutenant Kroll.

"Well, whether it's so or not," he said, "you weren't married to her were you, son?"

The lieutenant shook his head.

"No," he answered, "but what difference does it make?"

"If you don't understand," Briggs said, "it won't do any good to tell you."

The lieutenant's face looked redder.

"I think you sound old-fashioned, sir," he said.

"That's an easy way to put it," Briggs began, but Daisy did not let him finish.

"Now don't you two start quarreling," she

said quickly. "It's all perfectly decent. I'm going out to Reno. Have you got the tickets, darling?"

"Yes," Lieutenant Kroll said. "I've got them."

"Now please don't be mean about it." Daisy put her hand on Briggs's arm again and looked up at him. "It's a sort of a mess all right but you *know* it will be better if you tell Boysie. It won't hurt so much."

"He dished it out, sir," Lieutenant Kroll said. "He's got to take it."

Briggs walked to the door.

"Well, good-by," he said. "I hope he'll think he's lucky."

That was what came of knowing people too well and liking them too much. The sordid little tale was on his hands. By accident and beyond all help he would have to retail all of it to Lieutenant Boyden. He would have to see the change come over Boyden's face and watch him take it. He had thought that he was tolerant and knew the world. He never thought he could feel so unhappy over something that was no real concern of his.

VIII

New York was a very rear area compared to San Francisco. The war tide swirled up and down the streets of San Francisco like the tide in the Golden Gate. Marines and sailors dozed in the hotel lobbies, and everyone was taking a last drink before leaving, or a first drink on coming back. In the room at the St. Francis on the night before Briggs left for Pearl, everyone knew what had happened to the *Rogue River*, although it was not yet in the papers for reasons of security. Personally, Briggs could not see much use in the delay when so many people knew of it already, and what was left of the *Rogue River* was back at Pearl and her surviving crew were landed.

"Some damage was suffered by certain units" the communiqué had said. Briggs had heard about it in Washington, a week before he left, from a friend of his in Naval Personnel, but news was like waves from a stone thrown into water — the nearer you came to the spot the more you heard. The captain and the two commanders who sat in his room at the St. Francis knew him well enough to talk freely. The carriers were usually the ones that caught it, particularly when there was an overcast, and the *Rogue River* had been under intermittent attacks for days. A Zeke had come out of the overcast, flying low, and had made for the superstructure when a five-inch shell made it swerve and crash on the flight deck among the planes. The explosion had smashed through to the hangar deck and the ship had been on fire for an hour. It had taken nearly all the ocean to put it out, the captain said. It was surprising to think that anything like the *Rogue River* could have got back under her own power. Of course, there had been casualties and men trapped below deck but, though it would take quite a while to patch her up, she made port. They spoke quietly in technical terms, much as he had heard doctors discuss a case of thrombosis.

"They used to say she was a lucky ship," Briggs said.

"Yes," the captain answered, "but no ship stays lucky all the time."

Briggs was thinking of the wardroom of the *Rogue River*, of the officers drinking coffee and listening to the phonograph, reading, or writing letters. He was thinking of Boyden sitting at a bridge game, and of the annoying way he slapped down his cards, particularly when he took a trick.

"Hey," he heard them say. "What are you playing — slapjack, Boysie?"

"Hell," he heard Boyden answer, "I want to know it when I take 'em."

Of course there was a casualty list, but no one there had seen it.

The captain had heard that a group of the fliers had just been briefed and a lot of them were by their planes when the Zeke had crashed.

"There was a flier," Briggs said, "named Boyden — James K. Boyden."

"If he's alive, you'll see him," one of the commanders said. "Those kids all went to Pearl."

That was all there was to say about Boyden. He was nothing but a name, and he had been checked off on the record.

"He was a very nice kid," Briggs said. "His wife's leaving him. He doesn't know it yet."

"Those kids are always mixed up," the captain said. "They always marry some little floozie before they think about it. Now when I was in Jacksonville there were two kids . . ." the captain's voice went on and Boyden's name and personality were gone.

Human values and relationships were changing already. It was infinitely simple going back. He knew exactly what he would find there and how everyone would behave. The preoccupations and reserves of home were gone already — tied up in a package and checked somewhere, to be called for later. Possessions, insurance, old friendships, money in the bank, old ambitions, how to educate the children, whether to sell the house or not, whether to move or not — all these things were packed away and the memory of them was growing uncertain.

Yet they were not entirely forgotten. The commander was explaining how much gas his car used back at home, and the captain had been very lucky in raising delphiniums. The way he did it, he said, was by giving the matter a little study. He did not just go around and ask the neighbors how to raise delphiniums.

It was refreshing to speak of such extraneous subjects but it was much more important to know what to take with you. The clothing situation was not bad at all in the West Pacific. There were plenty of shoes at Guam, but it was hard to get shaving soap in sticks. It was a good idea to take some good sun glasses and a decent fountain pen. You could get everything else at Guam. If you had any room in your luggage, it was good to take along some Scotch. That would help you more than any other equipment, Scotch and something to read, if you didn't want to spend all your spare time with paper-covered books.

"Well," the captain said, "we'd better turn in. The car will take us to Alameda at six."

"You say those fliers on the *Rogue* are back at Pearl?" Briggs asked again.

"Yes," the commander answered, and he yawned. "They're waiting there for orders."

"God, they must be tearing that room to pieces next door," the captain said. "They're really taking it apart. I hope we can get some sleep."

The beauty of it was that you could do nothing much about it. William Briggs was aware of a relief when he boarded the plane next morning. There was so much one could forget for a while when the motors began turning.

The weather over the bay was overcast, so that it was hard to see the city when they circled for altitude, but once they were an hour offshore they were in the morning sun and the sea was blue beneath them, and home was left in space. Now that they were moving toward the islands, he could think of Boyden and his problems in a very different way. It might be that Boyden was already gone and that he would never know what had happened back at home, gone with all his simple thoughts, never to receive the messages which Briggs was carrying.

"Just tell him that we all love him," Mrs. Boyden was saying. He remembered that she was crying when she said it. "That's what he'll need most. He'll need a mother now."

It still seemed to him doubtful, but it was just as well that she thought he would.

"Don't listen to them when they tell you not to tell the truth," Susie was saying. "He'll know it's better, when he knows the way it really is."

"Tell him we're looking after everything," Mr. Boyden was saying. "He doesn't need to worry about any of the details. Tell him we've got a good lawyer. Make him understand that everybody is on his side and be sure he doesn't blame himself. Tell him this sort of thing is happening all the time."

"Tell him how much better it is," Daisy was saying, "than if we went on without my really loving him. It's the only way that's honest. Tell him that."

"Tell him that he is only a kid after all," Mr. Boyden said. "We all make mistakes at his age."

"Tell him we love him," Mrs. Boyden was still crying. "Tell him that it will all be just as though it never happened."

"Tell him . . . tell him . . ." they were saying. "Tell him he has all his life to live."

Briggs remembered what the chaplain had said on the transport at Guam, but there was no way of explaining to the Boydens that their son might

have lived a good many lives already and that anyone like Boyden might easily grow tired of living.

Briggs began repeating to himself, as he had a
great many times before, the sort of speech that
he would have to make.

"Listen, son," Briggs would say, "there's been a
little trouble back at home. Not anything that is
going to hurt you indefinitely, but you'd better
hold onto your seat and brace yourself. Just remember this sort of thing is always happening. . . ."

It was three quarters of an hour before sundown
when the plane approached the air base. First
he saw Diamond Head and the palms along Waikiki
Beach, then the docks and houses of Honolulu.
The rain clouds hung over the mountains but all
the shore was bathed in sunlight. The whole island
was a map of mottled greens — except for the
gashes made by the supply dumps and the airstrips.
He had a glimpse of Pearl Harbor full of shipping
and then all the airfield installations and the rows
of planes. He watched the nervous expression on
a flier's face beside him as they waited for the
wheels to touch. Those boys were always critical of
any other pilot's work.

When he stepped to the ground he started straight for the enclosure where the incoming passengers would be checked, without bothering to look around him, and he almost ran into Lieutenant Boyden before he saw him.

He was not even sure that he expected to see Boyden at all. He had thought of inquiries and delays and of long waits while officers consulted files. At any rate, whatever he had been thinking, the sight of Boyden was a shock. His face leaped out at Briggs from the faces of a group of officers who were standing in front of the Administration Building.

"Hey," Lieutenant Boyden said, "what's the matter? Don't you know me, Pops?"

His shirt was riding out of his trousers. His tie had slid a trifle sideways. The uppers were cut from his boots and his socks sagged over them. It was Boyden's way of showing, without using ribbons, that he was in the category of old fliers who came from places where dress was not important. Everything about Boyden was exactly as Briggs remembered, the way he held his head, the way he shook hands.

"I never thought I'd see you here," Briggs said.

Boyden smiled and shrugged his right shoulder and pushed his shirt beneath his belt.

"Why, hell — I've been waiting for you," he answered. "They let me call home the other night. Daisy's phone was disconnected but I got the folks." Boyden cupped his hands in front of his mouth. "Hello, Papa. Hello, Mama. Hello, everybody. This is Jimmy back for a little rest, and loving everything. How's tricks, everybody? . . . The word was you might be in tonight. Cripes, I'm glad to see you, Pops." Boyden slapped him on the back. "They say Daisy's away visiting, but they say you saw her, Pops."

"Yes," Briggs began.

"She's a cute kid, isn't she?" Boyden said. "I got you a corner room at the Hotel. If you want service around here, just ask Boyden. I've got a jeep. Where's that driver? Hey — where are you, Chief?"

They walked through the building out to the parking space and a chief petty officer carried the bags. He tossed them onto the jeep and they climbed in beside them. Boyden was still talking.

"Downtown, Chief," Boyden was saying. "It

seems that some of us kids need a little rest and relaxation, Pops. It seems we're a little tired." But there was no sign of strain on his face.

"We just got in a week ago," Boyden was saying. "Boy-oh-boy! And we start in next Monday at Barber's Point breaking in new kids. Boy-oh-boy! You should have been there, Pop."

They were on the road to Honolulu, with the sky behind them red from the sunset. They were moving past the supply dumps and the Marine camp. The sound of the traffic rose in waves around them, so that it was hard to talk.

"Everything looks about the same," Briggs said.

"Sure," Boyden answered. "How else do you think it would look?"

There were the same trucks, the same busses, the same tents, the same heaps of ammunition, the same military police, the same shacks and open shops as they neared Nuuanu stream, and the same crowds of soldiers and sailors — drifting through the streets.

"We'll eat at the Outrigger," Boyden said.

"All right, son," Briggs answered.

Now that the first minutes were over he and

Boyden seemed to have been together for a long while.

"But first we'll get squared away and have a drink." Boyden was looking at him through the gathering dark. "You sound kind of tired, Pops."

"It's the plane," Briggs said. He still felt the vibration of the plane. "I'm glad to see you, son. You're all right, aren't you?"

"What the hell," said Boyden. "I'm always all right. Say — "

"What?" Briggs asked.

"You should have been aboard. Oh, baby. You missed it, Pops."

It must have been pretty bad if it still intruded upon Boyden's thoughts.

"I hope you'll tell me about it tonight," Briggs said.

"Boy-oh-boy!" Boyden said, and he began to laugh. "Do you remember Jonesy?"

Briggs tried to think but he could not remember anyone named Jonesy.

"Comical things happen," Boyden said. "The blast lifted us both right up and we landed sitting down facing each other. It's comical the way those things happen."

"It must have been bad," Briggs said.

"Hell," Boyden said. "It's just some more of the same damn thing. Did you bring any Scotch out, Pop?"

Boyden was right — war was nothing but a repetition, a series of the same anecdotes that grew monotonous with the telling. The phenomena of explosion and of gunfire never varied. Fires burned in the same manner and ships sank like other ships. Infantry took the same sort of cover and planes fell in flames through the same pull of gravity. One could take that repetition just so long, and then finally one grew tired. It was not a weariness induced by fear as much as by boredom — the weariness of complete acceptance. They had even coined a word for it, and the word, oddly enough, was "happy." One got bomb-happy or slap-happy if one stayed too long, and there came a slowing of reflexes and a mechanical dull indifference. It seemed to Briggs that Boyden was near the edge of it — though externally he looked just the same.

"Let's see," Boyden said when they were in the hotel. "I've got the key. I'm using the other sack here. I hope you don't mind, Pop."

The windows of the hotel room were open and

the sound of the surf came up to them. Briggs could still see the outline of Diamond Head before Boyden switched on the lights.

"Come on," Boyden said, "break out that Scotch." He held the bottle in his hand, turning it slowly, peering at it from every angle. "Cripes," he said. "Black Label. That's worth about fifty bucks downtown. If you want something enough, it doesn't matter what you pay for it, does it?"

"No, as long as you're sure you really want it," Briggs answered.

"Nuts," he said. "If you want a thing enough, you're sure you want it, at least in my experience, and to hell with later, Pop."

It was only a step to the Outrigger Club. They walked past the old Hawaiian woman who sat in front of the hotel selling her tuberose *leis*, past the bookshop and past the souvenir shop that was offering "things Hawaiian" — shells and gourds and pieces of tapa cloth and brooches, and grass-skirted dolls. Boyden slackened his pace, and frowned at the objects in the window.

"It's a very funny thing," he said.

"What's a funny thing?" Briggs asked him.

Boyden took a few quick steps before he answered.

"Looking at all that junk," he said. "I don't seem to get used to being here. I don't get the old wham-wham out of it; and the Outrigger hasn't got the old wham-wham. Do you see what I mean?"

"Listen, son," Briggs said, "you used to say you never bothered."

"Who said I was bothering?" Boyden asked. "It's a perfectly normal reaction. Everyone reacts like that for a while, but it's the timing. I still keep expecting to snap back."

The room upstairs at the Outrigger was already crowded with a few girls and a few civilians, but mostly naval officers.

"There are a lot of new kids here," Boyden said. "It makes me kind of tired looking at all these new kids — all full of the old wham-wham. It's a very funny thing. I keep thinking I'm back on the *Rogue*. It seems more real than here. It's taking longer to snap back."

As Boyden tried inexpertly to express himself, his words had a clumsy eloquence. He talked of the *Rogue River* as he ate. There had been a swell crowd of kids aboard and Boyden had been "in." He knew he had been in, as soon as that blast had landed him on the deck. When he got up and found he was all right, he knew he did not have to bother about himself. It was the other kids that bothered him.

"Seeing them shot down," he said, "is different from seeing a whole lot of kids catch it on deck; and kids shut in up forward, burning up — oh boy."

You had your mind on other things when the ready ammunition magazines began exploding, but cleaning up afterwards — oh boy! Boyden put his hands on the table and pushed his chair back. "Let's get squared away," he said, "and get back and polish off that Scotch."

Suddenly he seemed to be in a hurry to leave. It was almost as though he had seen someone he did not want to meet, but when they were out on the street again he walked more slowly.

"Gee," he finally said, "I'm sorry, for being in a mood. How are tricks in Orange, Pops?"

They were in the hotel elevator alone except for the Japanese elevator boy in his blue monkey jacket. Briggs knew of course that they would have to come to it eventually, but he wished that Boyden would not keep watching him.

"Orange?" Briggs said cheerfully. "Oh, yes, I'll tell you in a minute." The elevator door clicked shut behind them and they walked down the hall.

"I bet the old apartment was in a mess," Boyden said. "Daisy likes disorder. What was she wearing, Pop?"

An orchestra was playing downstairs, and Briggs could hear gay voices and the clink of ice through open transoms.

"She was wearing a pink silk wrapper and blue pajamas."

"That kid never gets out of pajamas, if she can help it," Boyden laughed, and took out the room key. "And how's the little number? Can he talk yet?"

"No, not yet," Briggs said, "but he's looking fine."

"Like his Pop," Boyden said. "I'd like to see that kid."

Boyden closed the door behind them and took off his shirt.

"Let's take the whiskey straight," he said. "It's too good for soda. Here's looking at you, Pops."

Briggs sat down heavily in an armchair.

"It was funny, hearing them the other night," Boyden said. "It all came through just as though they were in the room. It's funny thinking of you just seeing them and all of them just being there. When — " Boyden stopped and rubbed his hand over the back of his head.

"When what, son?" Briggs asked.

"That's the trouble," Boyden said, and he held up his glass and shook it. "I don't know just what. I've got a hunch that I'm not quite in. Something isn't quite right, is it? You'd better give me the word, Pops."

Boyden looped his thumbs in his belt and stood waiting, but he spoke again before Briggs had time to answer.

"You get a mood. You get so you know whether you're in or not. You'd better give me the word, Pops."

Briggs grasped the arms of his chair carefully.

"Listen, son," he began slowly, and his voice sounded unnatural. "I remember something you said once. You don't want to get to liking anyone too much."

Boyden pulled his thumbs more tightly against his belt.

"That's so," he said. "Not out here you don't. Because what good does it do?"

"You can't help it sometimes," Briggs said slowly. "I can't help it that I like you, son."

"Listen, Pop, I appreciate that," Boyden said gently. "Thanks a lot, but you don't have to take it this way. What's the word?"

There had been a time, Briggs remembered, when he had believed that experience had taught Boyden less than nothing, and now he felt that somehow, somewhere, Boyden had learned something that he had not. Suddenly Boyden seemed older than he and much wiser. Suddenly Briggs seemed to be the one who was in trouble.

"I want you to try to think," Briggs began again. "I want you to try and use your head and not your emotions. Just try — " Briggs squirmed uneasily in his chair and stood up. "Just try to remember . . . You're mighty young, son. I know the way this sounds to you, but I'm prettily nearly old enough to be your father." Briggs tried to smile but he could not. "In fact, I could have been your father if I had been married at around your age. We've been around quite a lot together, not in terms of time, but we've been around. I know the way this sounds but I want you to believe — "

"Hell," Boyden said, and his voice was very gentle. "Don't mind me, go ahead and spill it, Pop."

"Just try to get it through your head," Briggs said, "that nothing that happens to you at your age matters as much as it does later. There's always a chance at your age. I guess nature takes care of that. So you mustn't think what I'm going to tell you is going to be the end of the world. On the contrary," Briggs forced himself to smile, "maybe you're in luck. Maybe it's a good thing that this is happening to you now."

Boyden moved his feet a trifle further apart as though he were on a deck and compensating for the motion.

"*Roger*," Boyden said, very quietly. He was using the flier's phrase of complete agreement. "I knew I had a hunch . . . Has Daisy been cheating, Pop?" No definite expression was left on Boyden's face. It was impossible to perceive the slightest indication of how he must have felt.

"Yes, that's it," Briggs said. He paused, but Boyden's face was still intent and blank. "There isn't any way of keeping it from you. I wish I didn't have to tell you, son."

Boyden moved very slowly to a straight-backed chair. He leaned one hand against it, and then he sat down slowly as though a sudden lurch might disturb his balance.

"*Roger*," he said. "I've got it. *Roger*. Don't take it so hard, Pops. You've shot the works. You're in. I'm taking over now. All you have to do is just tell me." He pointed to the whiskey bottle. "You'd better take a slug of that. You look as though you need it, Pops."

"Now, just try to remember," Briggs began, but Boyden raised his hand.

"No," he said. "Relax and take a drink first. I know this is tough on you, and thanks a lot."

"Tough on me?" Briggs repeated.

"Yes," Boyden said. "Let's keep this straight. This is one place and Orange is another. Let's try not to mix them." Boyden put his hands on his knees and his shoulders relaxed. "It doesn't pay to like any guy too much. Don't think about me and don't pull your punches, Pop."

Briggs had never realized till then that Boyden really did live by a few simple phrases. Boyden was wiser than he, or at least he had achieved a working philosophy. Again Briggs felt as if he were telling his own troubles to an older man. Boyden listened, nodding sometimes, speaking sometimes.

"Boy," he said once. "Oh, boy," and he rubbed the back of his head.

His eyes narrowed slightly when he heard of Lieutenant Kroll.

"So that's the guy," he said. "Well, well. I thought he turned her down. Well, well."

But Daisy had asked how anyone could make such a lousy crack as that.

Most of the time Boyden sat quietly listening and Briggs could think of his words as sinking like stones into Boyden's silence. He remembered what Boyden had said about his thoughts before he went to sleep, about home and when he was a kid, and the apartment on Maple Street — the third house down, the only double stucco house with the tree in front of it, a kind of weeping something. And when Boyden had thought of luck, he had thought of himself and Daisy. (You got to know what love was, living in little shacks and one-night stands.) And sometimes before he went to sleep he had thought about that ride he and Daisy had taken in that jalopy up from Florida, when nothing had been wrong, not for a single minute.

All this, Briggs knew, must be lying somewhere in the depths of Boyden's silence, all made the more intense because he was so young. And Briggs could think of his words falling and breaking all those thoughts which he had once considered banal and mediocre. He could hear the surf through the open window when he had finished.

"*Wilco*," Boyden said. "*Wilco. Out.*" He was speaking in naval parlance acknowledging an order. His voice was like a hundred other voices that Briggs had heard on the radio speaker at sea, and there was the same finality and the same incisiveness in that word "out" that meant those voices were gone, perhaps forever.

"Say," Boyden said suddenly. "What about Verna May? Did you happen to see her, Pops?"

There still was Verna May. Perhaps he was thinking that that might have been real love after all.

"She's engaged," Briggs said. "That friend of yours — Sam Tilton."

"The hell you say!" Boyden said. "Oh boy. Well, *Wilco — Out*."

And he seemed to be gone like those radio voices although he was just a few feet away.

"I'm sorry, son," Briggs said. "Now don't take it too hard. Just remember you made a mistake about Daisy. Anyone makes mistakes."

Boyden looked up at him.

"You're a good guy, Pops," he said, "but don't be too hard on Daisy. Poor kid. If I had been around — " Boyden shook his head, "but I wasn't around. Poor kid . . . Just remember it's happening all the time. Kids get mixed up in a war, I guess — particularly around an airstrip. It's in the atmosphere, I guess."

It was Boyden's voice, but they were very nearly Daisy's words and to Boyden they seemed to explain everything. Boyden stood up and scratched himself.

"Say, I wonder if I've got the itch," he said. "Don't let it worry you. This doesn't get me, Pop. Now there's the kid — "

"What kid?" Briggs asked. Boyden's indiscriminate use of the word confused him.

"My kid," Boyden said. "Say, he can get the full allotment now. Does he look like me, Pop?"

"Your mother says he does. Personally, I wouldn't know," said Briggs.

"Don't get sore," Boyden said. "What do you want me to do, cry?"

Briggs realized that a sort of bewildered exasperation must have been reflected in his voice.

"You see, it doesn't get me," Boyden said again. "It's just as though it had happened to some other kid. It was so long ago, do you see? Some other kid, not me. So much keeps happening. They really run you ragged in this war." Boyden looked at his watch and shook it and held it to his ear. "The damn thing keeps stopping. How many hundred is it?"

"It's after ten," Briggs told him. "We can't go out. We haven't got a pass."

"All right, all right, we can do it tomorrow,"

Boyden answered. "I was just thinking. . . . There's the cutest little trick — "

"What sort of a trick?" Briggs asked, and Boyden corrected himself.

"The cutest little kid. It's funny the way things happen, isn't it?" Boyden said. "I met her yesterday at the U.S.O. She lives up at Pacific Heights. Say, you've got to meet her. She's really a cute trick. It's funny the way things happen, isn't it, when there's a war on?"